Having Her Boss's Baby

SUSAN MALLERY

All the characters in this book have no existence outside the imagination of the author, and have no relation whatsoever to anyone bearing the same name or names. They are not even distantly inspired by any individual known or unknown to the author, and all the incidents are pure invention.

First published in Great Britain 2007
Large Print edition 2007
Silhouette Books Limited, Eton House,
18-24 Paradise Road, Richmond, Surrey, TW9 1SR

© Susan Macias Redmond 2006

ISBN-13: 978 0 263 19857 7

Set in Times Roman 16¾ on 20¼ pt.
35-0507-60700

Printed and bound in Great Britain
by Antony Rowe Ltd, Chippenham, Wiltshire

SUSAN MALLERY

is the bestselling and award-winning author of over fifty books for Harlequin and Silhouette books. She makes her home in the Los Angeles area with her handsome prince of a husband and two adorable-but-not-bright cats.

Chapter One

Until Noelle Stevenson actually saw the word "pregnant" on the plastic stick, she'd allowed herself to believe everything was going to be all right. After all, it had been her first time. Wasn't she supposed to have a grace period? Like when a light bill was due? Those extra couple of days until disaster struck?

Apparently not, she thought, barely able to breathe as she turned the plastic over in her hands. Pregnant. *Her.*

She couldn't imagine what her parents were

going to say. Not that they would kill her. Anger seemed pretty manageable. Instead they would get quiet, look at each other in that way of silently communicating that had always driven her and her sisters crazy, then ask her what she wanted to do. After all, she'd created the situation, now she would have to deal with the consequences. They were going to be disappointed and that was always the worst.

Noelle looked in the mirror and saw the fear in her eyes. She wouldn't be twenty for another two weeks. She was supposed to be starting her second year at community college in the fall. There couldn't be a baby. This wasn't really happening.

The sound of footsteps on a hardwood floor got her attention. It was barely after six in the morning. The office should have been deserted. Who had picked *this* particular morning to come in early, too?

Not waiting to find out, Noelle stuffed the stick back into the box and shoved the box into her coat pocket. She quickly glanced around the private bathroom of her employer to make sure she hadn't left anything behind, then hurried through his office, hoping to make an escape before anyone caught her.

She raced across the large space and dashed into the hall, only to slam into the one person she would most like to have avoided.

"What's the rush?" Devlin Hunter asked as he reached out to steady her.

Noelle cleared her throat, then forced herself to smile as she stepped back and wondered what on earth she was going to say. The truth was impossible. She could imagine the look on his face if she blurted out, "Gee, Mr. Hunter, I needed to come in extra early so I could have some privacy in the bathroom. At home, I share with my three sisters. What with me thinking I might be pregnant with your late brother's child, I really didn't want to let my family in on my little secret. You, either, for that matter."

"Um, no rush," Noelle said, knowing she sounded impossibly stupid. "I, ah, needed to get some work done, so I came in to get a jump start on it."

Mr. Hunter glanced at his watch, then at her. "It's barely after six."

"I actually know that."

"*I* didn't know Katherine was such an exacting boss," he said, a faint smile tugging on the corners of his mouth.

Technically, Noelle didn't work for Mr. Hunter. She worked for his assistant. Secretary to an assistant—it was a little like being the dog's pet. Still, she adored Katherine, who always let her schedule her hours around her college classes.

"She's not," Noelle said. "I just wanted to, you know, be diligent."

"Admirable."

He studied her as if he didn't quite believe her. Noelle knew she was a lousy liar and wondered what, exactly, he could read in her eyes.

Mr. Hunter was tall—taller than Jimmy had been. They both had dark hair, but Mr. Hunter had green eyes, while Jimmy's had been brown. That wasn't the only other difference, either. Jimmy had been a lot younger and not nearly as responsible. Not until he'd gone into the army.

She didn't want to think about Jimmy being gone or her being pregnant. So she smiled and started to move around Mr. Hunter.

"I'll just get to my desk," she said, hoping he wouldn't ask why she'd been in his office.

"All right."

She moved to the left and he moved to the right. As they were facing each other, that meant they bumped. He excused himself and lifted his briefcase so she could get by. The corner of the case nudged her pocket and something fell to the floor. Mr. Hunter bent down and picked it up.

Her heart froze in her chest. One second there was beating and the next…nothing. She closed her eyes and willed herself to disappear. Or at the very least, grow wings and fly away. Flying would be excellent.

Instead there was only the sound of their breathing and a long, lingering silence.

"Did I interrupt you before or after you took the test?" he asked quietly.

She kept her eyes shut. Humiliation burned both inside and out. "After."

"And?"

She opened her eyes and looked up at him. "I'm pregnant."

Dev had figured the worst part of his day would be arguing with one of his suppliers. He'd been wrong.

"Then I guess we should talk," he said and led the way into his office.

Pregnant.

Devlin swore silently. Jimmy had just been a kid, he thought grimly. Noelle Stevenson was even younger. He set the pregnancy-test kit box on his desk.

She sat across from him, all wide-eyed and scared. He doubted she could look more embarrassed or uncomfortable and guessed she wanted to be anywhere but here, which was exactly how he felt. But despite the awkward situation, he wasn't going to walk away from his responsibilities.

He'd always been the one to take care of his brother when they'd been younger and clean up Jimmy's messes when they were older. But a baby…

"You were dating my brother," he said.

She nodded without looking at him. "We'd been going out a couple of months when he joined the army. He said I should see other people after he went away, but I didn't want to, so when he came home on leave, he said…" She swallowed. "We talked about getting married."

Dev remembered being twenty and interested in a girl, and he knew his brother. If discussing marriage was what it took to get her into bed, then that's what Jimmy would have done.

"I thought…" She toyed with the buttons on her jacket. "He was really sweet and fun and he was going to a dangerous part of the world. He said he might not come back."

Dev held in a groan. Not just for the overused line, but with the realization that not only had his brother gotten a girl pregnant, that she might have been a virgin.

"Your first time?" he asked bluntly.

Noelle hunched over so her long, pale blond hair covered her face, but he saw her nod. Disbelief blended with anger. If his brother had been alive, Dev would have beaten the crap out of him. But Jimmy was gone. One way or another Jimmy had always managed to make his problems Dev's problems. This time, under circumstances that were still filled with grief. Pain warred with guilt but neither won. And there was still Noelle to deal with.

He figured it would be insensitive to boot up his computer at that moment so he could get into the personnel files there. Without them, he knew very little about her. She worked for his assistant. She'd been with the company a little less than a year. She'd had minimal office skills when she'd arrived, but she'd worked hard and now Katherine claimed she couldn't exist without her.

Sometime over the spring, Jimmy had met her and they'd started dating. But who was she and what the hell was he supposed to do now?

"I didn't mean for this to happen," Noelle said quietly, still not looking at him. "I thought I loved him, but I wasn't sure. And he was so sweet… But I knew I should wait. Only then he was killed and I thought I'd done the right thing. I felt so horrible for him and for you. I know you're his only family. And then I thought everything would be okay. Except I was late and a couple of days ago I realized I might be…you know."

She stopped and sucked in a breath. It was then he figured out she was crying.

He stood and walked into the bathroom, where some mystery cleaning person always left a fresh box of tissues. After handing them to her, he perched on the edge of his desk.

"How old are you, Noelle?"

She took the tissues and wiped her face with one, then blew her nose. "I'll be twenty in a couple of weeks."

Still a kid herself, he thought. "You go to college?"

"Community college. I'll start my second year in the fall." She wrinkled her nose. "I know, I know, I should be at UC Riverside, but early in my senior year of high school I was skiing with the youth group." She looked up and actually gave him a little smile. "I had a close encounter with a tree. I usually do better than that. Anyway, I broke my leg and messed up some ligaments, which meant surgery and physical therapy and more surgery. My mom homeschooled me and I was able to graduate with my class, but I missed out on a lot of activities and the SATs. I wasn't even able to apply to a four-year college. So I'm doing it this way, which is good because it saves a lot of money. I mean, there are four of us and it's not like my parents are rich or anything."

Too much information, he thought, not sure where to go first. "You still live at home?"

"Yes. I'm one of four girls. The oldest." The humor in her blue eyes faded. "Talk about setting a bad example."

"What do your parents do?"

"My dad's the pastor at our church and my mom works in the office."

Dear God, Jimmy had slept with a minister's daughter?

"What do you want to do when you finish college?"

"Go into nursing, specializing in pediatrics." She held up her hand. "I beg you, do not give me the 'be a doctor instead' lecture. When I was in the hospital, the people who made a difference for me were the nurses. That's what I want to do—take care of kids and help them be less scared while they're sick."

"No lectures," he promised.

Now what? The young woman was pregnant with his brother's child, and that made her his responsibility. But how to handle things? If Jimmy were still alive, he could insist they get married. He could…

Jimmy wasn't alive, he reminded himself again and he, Dev, was the reason.

The ever-present guilt coiled around him like a large, deadly snake. He willed himself not to react. The more immediate problem was Noelle's pregnancy and what to do about it, and her.

Noelle shifted uncomfortably in the chair. While she appreciated how nice Mr. Hunter was being, she didn't know what, exactly, he wanted from her. He wasn't the father of her baby, so this wasn't his problem. Still, at least he hadn't questioned her for saying Jimmy was the father and she didn't think he'd thought anything bad about her.

A baby. She touched her hand to her stomach. It didn't seem possible that there was a child growing inside of her. Sure, she'd always wanted a family, but not like this and not so soon. Except, with Jimmy dead, the baby was all that was left of him.

She wondered what he would have said if she could have told him. Despite his emotional proposal the last time he'd been home, she wasn't sure he would have wanted to go through with the marriage. She wasn't even sure she would have. Everything had happened so quickly. They'd been dating and having fun, then he'd been gone and they'd kept in touch with letters and e-mail and then he'd been back for just a short period of time. She hadn't been able to think.

"We should get married."

At first Noelle was sure she hadn't heard the words correctly. She looked at Mr. Hunter, trying to figure out if he'd really spoken.

"Excuse me?"

His gaze never left her face. "We should get married as quickly as possible. Jimmy was my brother. That makes the baby my responsibility.

I'm only doing what he would have done. The difference being, we aren't involved."

His responsibility? Technically he was the baby's uncle, she thought frantically, but in reality he was Mr. Hunter, her boss's boss and someone she didn't know at all.

"I'm suggesting a marriage of convenience," he added calmly. "Something temporary for, say, two years. Long enough for you to get on your feet and get used to being a mother. Then we would divorce. You'd get what Jimmy would have inherited, if he'd lived. I would like to continue to have contact with the child and see him or her raised as a Hunter, but otherwise you would be free to live your life."

"You're suggesting marriage and divorce," she said, amazed she could speak at all. Her brain whirled and twirled until she was so dizzy she couldn't imagine standing ever again. This was not happening. Mr. Hunter proposing? "You barely know me, Mr. Hunter. I don't know you at all. We can't get married."

He crossed his arms over his chest. "I'm not trying to seduce you, Noelle. While we will live in the same house, our lives will be entirely separate. I want to help you. I am Jimmy's only relative so his child is my responsibility."

That made sense, but marriage? Why hadn't he just offered child support? "I don't want to get married only to get divorced," she said. "I don't believe in that. I think marriage is a serious and permanent commitment."

"Which you can have later," he said. "With someone else. Someone you meet and fall in love with. I'm going to be blunt, Noelle. You're going to be twenty when the baby is born. You work part-time and you're attending college. From what you've said, your parents aren't very well-off. Can they afford to take on another child? Do you want them to? What about your dreams of being a nurse? How are you going to care for a baby, support yourself and the child and attend college? What about paying rent, bills, health insurance, college tuition? Do you really want to take this all on yourself?"

He leaned toward her. "I'm offering a temporary solution that allows you to get on with your life. All your expenses will be taken care of. We can hire a nanny to help out, if you'd like. At the end of the prearranged time, you'll have enough money to take care of everything. If you live carefully, you won't need to work if you don't want to."

As her brain hadn't settled down, she didn't know what to think. "Why?" she asked. "Why would you do this?"

For the first time since he'd invited her into his office, Mr. Hunter wouldn't look at her. "Jimmy going into the military was my idea," he said at last. "What happened to him is my fault."

He spoke calmly, but she heard the pain in his voice and in his words. He blamed himself for his brother's death.

Her instinct was to go to him and offer

comfort. Instead she said, "You didn't fire the gun, Mr. Hunter. You didn't kill your brother."

He returned his attention to her and raised his dark eyebrows. "Under the circumstances don't you think you should call me Dev?"

"What? Oh. Sure. Dev." Right now weren't names the least of their problems? "My point is you're not responsible for your brother's death and you're not responsibles for me being pregnant." As if Mr. Hunter—Dev—would ever be interested in her that way. She'd seen a couple of the women he'd dated. They were all tall, slinky, exotic beauties. She looked more like a Wisconsin farmgirl—all blond hair and freckles.

"I'm very serious about my proposal," he said.

Because he felt responsible, she thought. He would. She knew a little about him because of what Jimmy had told her. Dev had been in high school when his mother died. Jimmy had been only six or seven. Their father had disappeared and their paternal grandfather had stepped in to take care of the two boys. Only he had died a few years later and Dev had raised Jimmy.

Her boyfriend had frequently complained about how strict he could be, but Noelle had always admired Dev for taking on the challenging task of raising a teenager. From the little she'd known about him, Jimmy hadn't made things easy.

But Jimmy was still the only family Dev had and with Jimmy gone, there was only the baby.

"You don't have to marry me to have a relationship with your brother's child," she said. "I would never keep you from him or her. I realize you won't want to take my word on that, so I'll sign something if you'd like."

"Is that what you think this is about?" he asked.

She straightened in the chair and met his gaze. "I'm young, but I'm not an idiot. I'm aware of all the difficulties in raising a child in my situation. This isn't what I would have chosen for my life path, but it happened and I'll deal with the consequences."

A good speech, she thought, hoping he couldn't tell how much she shook as she gave it. What she hadn't mentioned was the mind-numbing terror at the thought of actually having to take care of a baby by herself. He'd been right before. How would she pay for things? When would she have time to work and go to school? She was fairly confident her parents wouldn't toss her out onto the street, but their small house was already jammed full. Where would they put a baby?

He studied her. "You're not what I imagined," he admitted. "Most of Jimmy's girlfriends have been…"

"Airheads?" she asked lightly.

He grinned. "Exactly."

"I know. He told me. He said dating me was a sign of his willingness to grow up. I think it was more the whole 'bad boy, good girl' thing. Opposites attract and all that."

"As a good girl, you had a thing for bad boys?"

Noelle hesitated. Something about this topic

felt strange. Maybe it was discussing her dating habits with a man who'd just proposed, however businesslike he'd meant it.

"I was always curious," she admitted. "But I'd never dated one until Jimmy." She wrinkled her nose. "Everyone in high school knew who my father was, so guys were wary about messing with a pastor's daughter. The guys who did ask me out were always well-behaved." And she hadn't minded. It had made life easy.

"Until Jimmy," Dev said.

"Right."

He moved from the desk to the chair next to hers. After pulling it around so it faced her, he sat down and reached for her hand.

"Noelle, I want you to seriously consider my offer. I could simply give you money, but you're going to need more than that. I have a large house with plenty of room for you and the baby. If you're married, you won't have to deal with awkward questions." He shrugged. "I don't know what Jimmy told you about me, but I'm not such a bad guy. My vices are all pretty boring and I *will* take care of you and the baby. In a couple of years, or whenever you're ready, we'll divorce. You'll be financially stable and no longer dealing with a newborn."

She was as caught up in the fact that he was holding her hand as in what he was saying. His touch was gentle, yet firm. His skin warm. There was nothing sexual or romantic in the contact, but she was still very aware of him sitting so close to her.

She liked his determination. Her father had always said to look for a man who wouldn't give up. He was—

Wait a minute, she thought. Was she seriously considering his proposal? Was she thinking she would marry a man she barely knew simply to take his name and his money?

"I'm not like that," she said, pulling her hand free and standing. "I'm not mercenary."

Dev rose as well. "No one is saying you are.

Noelle, if Jimmy were still alive, wouldn't you expect him to marry you?"

She didn't want to answer that. In this century, in this society, who *really* got married because of a baby? But in her heart, she knew she would have expected it. And she would have accepted, despite any misgivings about the future of their relationship.

"But you're not Jimmy."

"Think of me as standing in for him. Doing what he would have done."

Would Jimmy have married her? She honestly wasn't sure.

"It's two years," Dev said. "Trust me, time moves quickly. Did your parents know you were dating Jimmy?"

"What?" The change in subject startled her. "Um, they knew I was seeing someone from work, but that's all."

"Then for all they know, it could be me."

She blinked at him. Of course there had been times when she'd kept the truth from her parents, or squeaked around the actual facts, but to lie like this felt wrong on too many levels. Yet she was tempted.

The baby existed and she would have to deal with that. Dev was offering her a way to minimize the damage with her family, while allowing her to be a single mother and still pursue her dreams. It was almost too good to be true.

"What do you get out of all this?" she asked.

"Jimmy's child gets the family name. I get to be a part of his or her life."

"You can have both of those without marrying me."

"I want to make this right," he told her. "I can't take back what was done, but I can do my best to help. You don't know me, Noelle, but you're going to have to trust me on that."

She wasn't sure much trust would be required. Devlin Hunter was the kind of man to get everything in writing. Which meant there would be paperwork.

"I don't want what Jimmy would have inherited," she said. "That's too much." Dev's company, Hunter Manufacturing was a massive, multimillion dollar business. "Maybe some child support and a house." She winced. Even that sounded too greedy. "Just the child support," she amended. "Jimmy would have paid that anyway."

Dev shoved his hands into his slacks pockets and smiled at her. "You're saying yes."

"Oh." She turned the idea over in her mind. "I guess I am." When had she decided this was what she wanted to do? Did it matter? Dev was right. Accepting his proposal made her life much easier.

She still wasn't sure what he got out of the deal. Unless it was to be part of a family again, even for a little while. But was that even important to him?

"I don't know you at all," she said.

"We'll change that," he promised. "Let's have dinner tonight. We can work out the logistics, set up a timetable and move forward."

That made it sound as if they were closing a business deal rather than discussing a marriage. And when she thought about it, she realized it was true.

"All right," she agreed. "Where do you want to meet?"

"My house." He moved around the desk and grabbed a piece of paper. After writing the address, he handed it to her. "Six-thirty?"

She took the paper and nodded. "Okay. I guess I should, uh, get back to work."

"You're not due in for another couple of hours."

"I know, but I'm already here." She walked to the door, then glanced back at him. "Thanks for everything."

"Thank you, Noelle," he said. "Don't worry more than you have to. We'll get this worked out. Everything will be fine."

She smiled and left. Fine? She was pregnant with her late boyfriend's child, she had just agreed to temporary marriage with a man she didn't know, for a bunch of reasons she couldn't remember, and she had big plans to lie about the whole thing to her family.

Fine didn't really cover it.

Chapter Two

Noelle left work shortly before noon. She'd already put in more than her usual amount of hours and cleared out her in-basket, which felt good. She'd been efficient, determined and focused. It had been the only way to get through the hours. If she allowed herself to stop moving, she would think about what had happened that morning. She would think about being pregnant and Dev's impossible proposal and she would lose it. Not something she wanted to do in front of all the women in the office.

So she kept a smile on her face and her mind on her work until she could escape to her car and drive home, where she knew she would find her mother. Funny how at nineteen, all she wanted was to run to her mom and be comforted. Maybe that need never went away. Yet in about eight months, she would have her own child to think about.

"Impossible," Noelle murmured as she drove out of the Hunter Manufacturing parking lot. "The entire situation is impossible."

How could she be pregnant? How could she consider marrying Devlin Hunter? While she couldn't change the former, she could work the latter. She'd been crazy to accept his proposal. Taking the easy way out was never smart, she reminded herself. She'd jumped at what he'd offered because it smoothed things over, but she knew better. And that was why she was so determined to get home. Her mother always left the church office for a couple of hours in the middle of the day. They would sit down and

Noelle would confess everything. Then her mother would tell her how to get out of her fake engagement with her boss.

Noelle knew that Dev would probably push back. He was that sort of man. But in time he would come to see that he could still be a part of his brother's child's life without going to the extreme of marrying her. While she would welcome child support, she wasn't going to insist on it. Somehow she would get by.

"Hey, Mom," she called as she walked in the back door of the two-story house she'd lived in since she was a kid. The place was old and a little run-down but homey and comfortable. She moved from the laundry room into the kitchen, where she found her mother sitting at the table.

"Hi, honey," the older woman said with a smile that didn't seem quite right. "I didn't expect you home for lunch."

"I got to work really early, so I finished early," Noelle said as she took a seat and smiled at her mother. It was only then that she noticed the other woman seemed to be brushing away tears. "Mom? Are you all right."

Her mother sighed. "I'm fine." She sniffed. "Okay, I'm a little weepy, but it's no big deal. Your father and I…" She swallowed. "We had a fight. We don't do it very often, so we're not good at it. Maybe we should take a class on the twenty-seven best ways to argue."

Her attempt at humor fell flat. Noelle touched her arm. "We never hear you and Dad fight. You get crabby from time to time, but not real arguments. Is everything okay?"

"It's fine. I told your father I'm tired of working in the church office. I want to do more. Meet other people. We're so insulated."

Noelle didn't know what to say. Her mother *loved* working in the church office. At least that's what she'd always said. For as long as Noelle could remember, her mother had talked about how lucky she was to work with great people and be part of a caring community.

"I thought it was what you wanted," she said at last.

"Well, it's not." Fresh tears filled her mother's eyes, then spilled down her cheeks. "Oh, I hate getting emotional. I need to do this. It's important."

"Why?" Noelle asked.

"Because… Because…" She drew in a breath, then shoved her hand into a pile of envelopes. "Because of these. Your father is so stubborn. He says the Lord will provide, and He does. Sort of. But there is also reality and helping one's self. I've always had to be the practical one in the relationship and I don't mind that. It's just when he makes things more difficult…"

Noelle bit her lower lip, but didn't say anything. Her mother had never talked to her like this before—as if she were an adult.

"There's not enough money," her mother said flatly. "There are too many bills. Your college hasn't been very much and when you transfer to UC Riverside, we'll be able to spring that, but

Lily's going to that private Christian university. Of course we're delighted she was accepted and they *will* provide some financial aid, but still… Then there was her graduation car."

A family tradition, Noelle thought, suddenly feeling guilty about the car she'd received the previous June when she'd graduated from high school.

"It adds up," her mother said quietly.

Noelle looked at the stack of bills. The corner of one caught her eye. "Is this from the hospital?" she asked as she pulled that envelope from the pile. "From my accident?"

Her mother took the bill and tucked it under the others. "Don't worry about it."

Noelle stared at her. "But we have insurance."

"It doesn't cover everything. I'm making payments. Believe me, that's the least of our financial problems."

Noelle wasn't so sure. "What about the physical therapy place? Are you still paying them?"

Her mother stood and crossed to the refrigerator. "What do you want for lunch? There's some lunch meat. We could make sandwiches."

Noelle felt her stomach tighten. She'd had no idea her parents were still paying for an accident that had happened nearly two years ago. How much had those bills been?

"Are you leaving your job in the church office to get a better-paying one?" she asked.

Her mother leaned against the counter. Jane had married at nineteen, given birth to her first daughter at twenty and had just turned forty the previous March. She looked much younger and strangers frequently expressed surprise that she could really have a daughter in college.

"The regular business not only pays more, the benefits will supplement the insurance we already have. I've been asking around and I have a couple of really good offers. I'm deciding which one to take. Unfortunately, your father sees this as some kind of defection."

Noelle wasn't so sure. "Maybe he's just sad he can't provide for his family the way he'd like."

"That, too," her mother admitted. "The male ego is a fragile organ." She frowned. "But it's not really an organ, is it? An instrument? An entity?" She gave a wry smile. "I don't even know what the male ego is and yet it is currently dominating my life."

"Daddy loves you. He wants you to be happy."

"I *am* happy," her mother said. "He's the most wonderful man. I wouldn't want to hurt him for anything. But we need to get a handle on the bills. Sometimes I think if there's one more unexpected expense, I'm going to run screaming into the night." She paused. "Is this too much, Noelle? I'm sorry. I probably shouldn't be sharing this with you. It's just lately you seem so grown-up and responsible. I feel as much like your friend as your mother."

Noelle stood and crossed to her mother. "It's fine," she said. "I'm glad you can talk to me. Everyone needs to be able to talk to someone."

They embraced. As her mother hugged her, Noelle fought tears of her own. Her secrets pressed upon her but she couldn't say anything now. Her mom didn't need one more thing to worry about.

"So—sandwiches?" her mother asked as she stepped back.

"Sounds great."

They worked side by side, then sat down to have lunch. Noelle chatted about work and her friends and was careful not to say anything about being pregnant or the deal she'd made with Dev. Now that she understood the financial situation at home, there was no way she could add a baby to the mix. Not with Lily going off to college this fall and Summer graduating from high school next year. Her parents couldn't possibly afford a baby and if Noelle tried to handle things on her own, they would only insist on helping.

She might not be happy about the deal Dev had offered, but right now it seemed the only way out.

"Thanks for meeting me on such short notice," Dev said as he walked into the office of Andrew

Hart, his attorney for the past ten years. Andrew had been Dev's grandfather's attorney for several years before that, ever since the elder Hart had passed away. A Hart lawyer had handled Hunter business since the company began, shortly after the end of the Second World War.

Andrew motioned to a leather sofa against the wall and walked to a wet bar in the corner. "What can I get you?" he asked.

"Nothing for me."

"All right." Andrew took the club chair across from the sofa. "What can I do for you?"

"I'm getting married."

Dev said the words aloud, but he had trouble believing them. Married. This time yesterday the biggest social event on his agenda had been thinking it was time to start dating again. He'd been between women for a few months and was feeling a definite itch. But any scratching was about to go on a very long hold, he thought grimly. Everything in his life would change as soon as he married Noelle.

"Congratulations," Andrew said, sounding a little surprised. "I didn't know you were seeing anyone seriously. I assume you want a prenuptial agreement."

Andrew was several years older than Dev, but still a friend. Dev wasn't about to keep the truth from him.

"Actually I want the opposite," Dev said. "We're only going to be married a couple of years. When we divorce, I want her to have an excellent settlement."

Dev paused, then laughed when he saw Andrew's shocked expression.

"I'm not crazy," Dev added. "Nor am I marrying for the usual reasons."

He explained about Noelle dating Jimmy and the subsequent pregnancy.

"No offense, but you *are* crazy," his lawyer told him. "Give her some money. Set up a trust fund for the kid. You don't have to marry the girl."

"I want Jimmy's son or daughter to have the family name," Dev said stubbornly. "I want to make sure Noelle is taken care of. She's not even twenty yet and her father's a minister. It was her first time and Jimmy talked her into bed by claiming he wanted to marry her."

"That was Jimmy, not you. As your attorney, I have to insist that you—"

Dev shook his head. "Talk to me as a friend, not an attorney."

"Then I still think you're crazy," Andrew said with a sigh. "But I'm not even surprised you want to do this."

"I'm doing what Jimmy would have done when he found out Noelle was pregnant."

"As your *friend*," Andrew said, "I doubt Jimmy would have been willing to go through with a quickie wedding."

Dev agreed with Andrew, but Jimmy wasn't here to prove either of them right or wrong. And Jimmy not being here was Dev's fault.

Dev had tried to do the right thing where his brother was concerned. Had tried and obviously failed. The baby gave him a second chance.

"I would have insisted," Dev said. "He would have married her. But he can't, so I will. Besides, I need to be sure Noelle is capable of being a good mother and that she's willing to take on the task. What better way to find that out than to observe her myself?"

"That's what private detectives are for." Andrew held up both hands. "I know I can't talk you out of this, so I'll draw up some paperwork."

"The plan is for us to be married for two years, then divorce. I want her to have what Jimmy would have had."

Andrew paled. "Half of everything? You're giving her half of the business? It's been in your family nearly sixty years. She's not entitled to half of the company. Community property laws are clear on that."

"Not ownership, but an income from the company. I also want a trust fund set up for the child. I'll fund it now and let it grow. Child support, a house equivalent to mine, plus a monthly allowance for upkeep."

Andrew swore. "Generous. I don't usually have clients trying to give money away at the end of a marriage."

"I do my best not to be ordinary."

"You're never that. I can have a draft ready in two days."

"That's fine. I don't know when the wedding will be, but I'll keep you informed."

Andrew hesitated, then said, "Dev, are you sure? You don't have to do this."

"I want to. Jimmy's child deserves this." So did Jimmy, but his brother was no longer around. All Dev could do was wait for the baby to be born and hope things turned out differently. That this time he wouldn't screw up.

Riverside had started out as a rural community. It was only in the past few years that it had become yet another bedroom community for the ever-growing Los Angeles and Orange counties. But even fifty years ago, there had been those with money and they had built several beautiful neighborhoods with elegant houses situated on massive lots.

Noelle found herself driving through one of those neighborhoods on her way to Dev's house. She'd never really been in this part of town before and she wasn't used to seeing houses with gates and servants quarters and such incredible landscaping. If not for the directions she'd gotten off the computer, she would have been totally lost.

Five minutes before their appointed meeting, she turned into a long driveway, past open wrought-iron gates toward a sprawling one-story house.

The lawn was the kind of green that only comes when one doesn't have to sweat the water bill. There were large, mature trees offering shady spots, and several pieces of sculpture for decoration. She saw a life-size casting of a boy and girl stretched out on a bench, each reading a book, and a young boy flying a bronze kite. In her neighborhood, lawn art tended toward pink flamingos, although a lot of people did put out seasonal wreaths or flags.

She parked, then stepped out of her car. The sweet scent of honeysuckle filled the air. The early evening was still and warm and quiet. This was a great place for kids, she thought, knowing she and her sisters would have loved the open spaces, although the elegant artwork would have been in danger of bodily harm.

She turned her attention to the one-story house and was grateful it didn't rise above her in cha-teaulike splendor. It might go on for miles and miles inside, but with only one level she knew it couldn't be too scary.

She walked up the stone steps and paused in front of a large, dark intimidating door. She hadn't known what to wear for her meeting with Dev. She hadn't wanted to be too casual, but this wasn't a date. In the end, she'd chosen a simple, light blue dress with tiny flowers and, despite the heat, a white jacket she'd borrowed from Lily. But even wearing more makeup than usual and high-heeled sandals, she still felt she should pop around back and use the servants' entrance.

Instead she knocked and waited until Dev opened the door.

"Noelle," he said with a smile. "Thanks for coming."

He motioned for her to enter the house, which she did, but speaking was out of the question.

She'd been so worried about what she was going to wear that she'd forgotten to think about what he might put on. Instead of the dark, elegant suits she was used to, he'd changed into jeans and a Hawaiian shirt. Okay, it was in muted colors and tucked in to show off his flat stomach, but it was still a Hawaiian shirt. There were flowers on it and lots of colors and he was her *boss*. Bosses like him didn't wear flowers!

She did her best to distract herself by turning her attention to the entryway. The walls were cream-colored and the floor was a dark, highly polished hardwood. To her left she saw an elegant formal dining room. To her right, closed French doors leading to an office or study.

There were carved moldings around the ceiling and elegantly framed paintings and photographs on the wall.

"Your home is lovely," she said, feeling both awkward and out of place.

"Thanks. I'm not taking any credit. My grandfather collected art and passed it on to me. My grandmother is responsible for all the antiques. The most I've done is to get a decorator in here to update a few of the rooms. But my idea of high-class is a jukebox and some sports posters."

She doubted that, but appreciated his effort to make her feel comfortable. Not that she could ever imagine that happening.

He led the way into a family room dominated by a huge old Spanish-style fireplace. There were large overstuffed sofas and comfy looking chairs. A built-in case held plenty of electronics, but she didn't see a television anywhere. She eyed the big painting over the fireplace and wondered if the TV was one of those expensive wall-mounted types, hiding behind art. If she knew Dev better, she would have asked, but as it was, she gingerly settled on the edge of a sofa cushion and wished she knew what to do with her hands.

"Do you want something to drink?" he asked. "Juice, soda, water?"

"Just water," she said.

"Okay. Be right back."

She jumped up to follow him, then sank onto the couch. Her heart pounded in her chest and her throat was so tight, she thought she might choke. If there had been any way out of the situation, she would have bolted for freedom. But all those doors seemed firmly closed, so she was simply going to have to figure out how to get through all this. Maybe in time things would get better.

He returned with a glass and a bottle of water. "Do you like Mexican food?" he asked.

She took everything and set it on the coffee table, then nodded. "Do you cook?"

He chuckled. "I make coffee and pour cereal in a bowl. This is from a great restaurant I've been going to for years. I picked up a little bit of everything, so you'll have a choice."

"Thank you."

She couldn't imagine ever eating again, what with the nerves dancing around in her stomach, but she could probably fake eating if she had to.

Dev sat at the other end of the sofa and faced her. "Noelle, I know this is a difficult situation for both of us. We're strangers who have agreed to get married for the sake of a child who is probably smaller than a grape right now."

The grape reference made her smile and some of her tension eased a little. At least he wasn't acting like all this was normal. She also appreciated that he was willing to take charge. Right now she couldn't imagine having to make a bunch of decisions about anything significant.

"So we'll go slowly," he continued. "We have some details to work out, and we'll get to them, but maybe we should just talk first and get to know each other."

"That's a good idea." She poured her water, then looked at the glass. "Only I have to tell you something first."

She risked glancing at him. He was handsome, she thought, which was interesting but not really important to the matter at hand. Still, if she had to look at a stranger over breakfast for the next two years, Dev was a nice-looking one. He was also kind and obviously loved his brother. More good news.

He waited patiently while she gathered her thoughts. She half stood, then sank back onto the sofa.

"I was going to tell you I changed my mind," she said, forcing herself to meet his dark gaze. "Nothing about this situation feels right to me. We're not in love. As you just said, we don't even know each other. While my pregnancy is a complication, it doesn't seem like a big enough one for us to go through with this. I meant what I said before—that marriage is an important and sacred commitment and one I take very seriously."

"You think I don't?" he asked.

"I didn't mean that, exactly," she said, desperately wanting to look away but refusing to.

"I do take it seriously," he told her. "I will honor our wedding vows, Noelle. This isn't a game to me."

"I didn't think it was a game," she said slowly, feeling that they were offtrack. She'd had a whole speech prepared and—

"It's not as if I'll be dating," he said.

Dating? She hadn't thought about that. He was a man who was used to being with women. Lots of different women. Maybe not at the same time, but still. She looked down and fought a blush.

"I didn't think about that," she admitted. "Your side of it. I… You've always had women in your life." Didn't he have to have those women for his needs? Weren't men supposed to have needs? In theory women had needs, too, but based on that single night with Jimmy, she couldn't imagine why they would want to acknowledge them.

"You're asking about sex," he said bluntly.

She swallowed, then nodded.

"I meant what I said," he told her, using her words. "I'm not doing this to seduce you."

She totally believed that. She wasn't his type at all. But if he wasn't going to sleep with her and he wasn't going to date, what was he going to do? Two years was a long time. She couldn't imagine him simply doing without.

But there was no way she could ask and they were completely off topic.

"I appreciate the no dating thing," she said. "It would be difficult to explain. But that's not what I wanted to talk about. I wanted to tell you that I'd changed my mind. That I wasn't willing to go through with this. I went home to talk to my mom and get her to help me figure out how to say all that."

She glanced at him and saw him watching her.

There was no way she could tell what he was thinking, which was probably a good thing.

"What happened?" he asked.

Noelle explained about the job change and the stack of bills. "They're still paying for my hospital stay and the physical therapy. I feel so horrible about that."

"It's not your fault," he said. "You didn't run into the tree on purpose."

"I know, but guilt is such a time-honored tradition. Anyway, I realized I couldn't burden them with another child. In a couple of years, I'll be on my feet and they won't have to worry about me." She glanced down at her lap, then back at him. "I'm taking the easy way out. I wanted you to know that."

Noelle spoke with a combination of shame and conviction Dev had never seen before. There had been no reason for her to confess all this to him. He wondered how much of her need to bare all came from her age and how much of it was who she was inside.

"This is me at my worst," she continued. "If you can handle that, we'll be fine."

She couldn't have found it easy to admit what she saw as her worst fault. How many other people would have been willing to be so honest? How many others would have simply taken what was offered?

Until this moment she'd been little more than the virgin Jimmy had knocked up. Suddenly she was a person, very possibly one he could respect.

"If this is as bad as it gets," he said gently, "we won't have any problem. Don't worry, Noelle, I have more than my share of faults. They're just not so easy to define."

Her blue eyes widened slightly. "I've just admitted I'm using you. How can that be all right?"

"You're agreeing to what I offered. There's a difference. I know exactly what I want and I'm getting it the best way I know how. You're not using me."

"But…"

He shook his head. "We're both going to come out ahead on this deal. You'll get to spare your family the expense of the baby and the embarrassment of their oldest daughter being pregnant and unmarried. I get to take care of my brother's child, be a part of his or her life and make sure the baby has the family name. It's a fair trade."

"Not for you," she said stubbornly. "This is costing you a lot."

"It's only money."

She stared at him. "How can you say that? It's a lot of money."

He shrugged. "Which I've always had. Giving some away isn't very meaningful because I've never done without. I work for a living, but only because I chose to."

"You say that as if you don't like what you do and you don't work hard. I've read the reports and you've doubled the size and the profits of the company since you took over. That doesn't happen by chance."

He was surprised she knew that. "My point is,

I've never done without so I won't miss what I give you. Don't make me out to be a hero, Noelle. I'm getting everything I want at very little cost to me. Don't forget that."

They had dinner in the kitchen. Noelle liked the round table next to the bay window and the view of the side yard, which was probably thirty or forty feet deep.

They shared fajitas, enchiladas, rice, beans and chips. Dev had a beer with the meal, but didn't offer her one. She wasn't surprised—not only was she underage, but she was now pregnant.

Pregnant—it didn't seem possible. She didn't feel any different. But she knew what had happened and her luck wasn't good enough for the test to be wrong.

"We have a lot of logistics to work out," he said. "But I think we've dealt with enough stress for tonight. Are you willing to put them off for a while?"

She nodded. No doubt his logistics were about

things like living arrangements and when they would get married. She could go a long time without dealing with those.

"I don't have any relatives," he continued, "but I will have to meet your family."

"I know," she said with a sigh.

"You could try to be a little enthused," he teased. "I don't eat with my hands."

She smiled. "I can see you have very nice manners. It's not that. It's just…everything. We're all really close and I don't know if I can fool them. I mean, they know I've been dating someone at work and my mom's been bugging me to bring him around, but why would they believe you're interested in me?"

He frowned. "Why wouldn't I be?"

She shrugged, not willing to say out loud that she wasn't all that special. "You're different from the other guys I've dated."

"Older, you mean."

"Well, that, too." She wondered if her parents could be tricked. "I'll write up some information on my parents and sisters for you. Just a few notes so you can convince them we've been together for a while."

"Good idea. I'll do the same about myself. We're going to have to act as if we're in love."

In love. He said the words so easily. She'd never said that to a man. How many times had he whispered the words to someone?

"What were you like growing up?" she asked instead of dealing with the love issue.

"I was a typical kid," he said. "I liked sports, didn't like school all that much, hated girls, had lots of friends." He smiled. "I got over the girl thing."

She smiled back. "I've heard."

"My mom died when I was sixteen and Jimmy was six. That changed things." His expression tightened. "My dad couldn't handle the pressure, so he took off."

"That's so sad," she said, not sure how any parent could abandon his children.

"My grandfather stepped in and he was great.

So I did okay, but it was harder for Jimmy. There was the big age difference. We'd still been close until Dad left. Then we grew apart." He took a drink. "Maybe he resented me taking over and being in charge. I don't know. The older he got, the less we got along."

Something about the way he told the story made her feel bad. As if he had regrets and they still hurt him. But before she could think of what to ask, the doorbell rang.

Dev glanced at his watch. "Right on time," he said as he stood. "Come on. You'll like this."

She had no idea what he was talking about but she followed him into the foyer. He opened the door and shook hands with a small, older man carrying a wide briefcase.

"Noelle, this is Frank Gaston. He owns Gaston Jewelry."

"Mr. Gaston," she said, shaking hands with him.

Mr. Gaston smiled at her, then turned to Dev. "She's very pretty. I hope you'll be happy together."

Dev smiled at her. "I'm sure we will be." He led the way into the dining room and indicated that Mr. Gaston should put his case on the table.

"I asked Frank to bring over a selection of engagement rings. I thought this would be easier than going to a store together." He moved next to her and lowered his voice. "Don't worry. You don't have to wear the ring until we've figured out how we're going to tell your family."

She nodded because speaking was impossible.

He was buying her an engagement ring? She'd only been pregnant since that morning. Okay, since she'd been with Jimmy, but she'd only *known* about it for fourteen hours. Everything was happening so quickly. She felt as if she were living her life on fast-forward. She wanted to slow things down and let her head stop spinning, but Mr. Gaston was already opening the case and asking her if she knew her ring size.

"Five, I think," she said, fighting the urge to tuck her hands behind her back. If she didn't accept a ring, maybe none of this would really happen.

But then Mr. Gaston held out a plain band to her and she found herself slipping it on her finger.

The band made it over her knuckle, but it was a tight fit.

"Five and a half," the older man said.

As she watched, he shifted through trays of stunning diamond engagement rings. They sparkled and winked and seemed to all be very large and impressive.

He removed a single tray and set it on the table. "All these are the right size," he said. "So, young lady. What do you like?"

There was nothing not to like, she thought, wishing she hadn't tried so hard to eat a little dinner. The fajitas were sitting heavily in her now tense stomach.

Dev stood next to her. "Not your style?" he asked in a low voice.

"They're lovely," she whispered back, "but they seem very expensive."

He chuckled, then kissed the top of her head. There was nothing romantic or sexual about the action, she thought, slightly stunned. It was something one would do to a favorite niece or cousin. Still, she felt comforted.

"Didn't we already have the money talk?" he asked. "Come here."

He took her hand and drew her to the table. She was so caught up in the feel of his warm, strong fingers touching hers that she didn't pull back when he picked up an emerald-cut solitaire and slid it onto her finger.

She'd imagined this moment since she'd been a little girl. The soft lights, the romantic music, the love in her husband-to-be's eyes as he slid the engagement ring on her finger. She'd never thought she would be in a strange house with a man she barely knew after agreeing to a two-year marriage of convenience while pregnant with another man's child.

Her life was practically a reality show.

"Not this one," she said, staring down at the stone. While it was beautiful, it seemed cold.

He took it off, but kept hold of her hand.

She let him, more aware of his touch than the rings. He picked up several different ones and put them back before finally taking a ring with a large center cushion-cut stone flanked by small baguettes.

"I think this one," he said as he slid it on. "What do you think?"

The ring was amazing. Pretty and big, without being gaudy. It seemed to suit the shape of her hand and her fingers. Which was all good, but it was still the biggest diamond she'd ever seen in her life.

"Will your insurance cover this?" she asked.

He laughed, then touched his free hand to her chin, forcing her to look at him.

"Do you like it?" he asked.

She didn't know what to say to that. How could anyone not like the ring?

"Can you stand to wear it?" he amended.

"Of course," she said quickly. "I didn't mean to imply—"

He cut her off with a shake of his head. "I know what you meant. Is this one okay?"

She nodded without looking at the ring. "You're being very generous."

"I know this is difficult," he said quietly. "Whatever happens, I want you to be happy."

She would never have imagined him saying something like that to her. For the first time since finding out she was pregnant, some of the fear faded and the future didn't look quite so bleak.

"I want you to be happy, too," she said.

"Good. Then we're agreed."

She wasn't sure if he meant the happy thing or the ring. Either way, she had the thought that maybe the next two years weren't going to be as difficult as she'd first imagined.

Chapter Three

"Why does the yarn always hate me?" Crissy asked as once again her project quickly tangled into a complete mess.

Noelle did her best not to laugh at her friend's distress. Crissy tried really hard in their knitting class, but it did seem as if she were always making a disaster instead of knitting the current project.

Crissy held up her two needles and the raggedy yarn falling off of one. "What am I doing wrong?" she asked, sounding both frustrated and near laughter.

Rachel leaned over and fingered the uneven stitches. "You're not even casting on right," she said. "Give it here. Let's start over and see if we can get this going."

Crissy handed over her needles, then winced as Rachel began unraveling everything.

Noelle carefully worked her needles, counting and making sure she kept up with the pattern. This was the first week of their intermediate class. They'd moved from simple squares and a shawl to a vest.

"Now cast on," Rachel said, leaning over Crissy's arm. "How many stitches do you want?"

Crissy looked at the pattern. "Twenty-five."

She worked laboriously, then grinned when she'd finished that first row.

"Much better," Rachel said.

Crissy beamed.

Noelle watched them, noting how Rachel's dark hair and Crissy's auburn curls looked against each other.

With everything else going on in her life,

Noelle had almost decided not to take the class, but now that she was here with her friends, she was glad she'd come.

She'd met Crissy and Rachel four months ago, when all three of them had come for their first class. Rachel had learned to knit as a teenager but hadn't picked up needles in years. Crissy and Noelle had been complete novices and totally uncoordinated. Lucky for them, Rachel had sat at their table and talked them through the first few lessons.

Soon they were meeting after class for a late dinner, as they did tonight. Noelle waited until they were seated in the small restaurant at the other end of the strip mall and had placed their orders before she spoke up.

"I have something to tell you," she said.

Instantly both Rachel and Crissy looked at her. "You've been a little quiet," Crissy said. "I'd wondered if something was up. Are you all right?"

Noelle nodded. She was close to her mom and

her sisters, but sometimes she wanted relationships outside of her family. While she didn't
know how she was going to break the news of
her pregnancy and marriage to her parents,
telling her friends didn't seem so scary.

"I'm going to have a baby," she said.

Her friends stared at her.

"Not tonight," Rachel said. "Because if you
are, I need to know. I'm starving and I'll eat fast."

Noelle laughed. "Not tonight. In about eight
months."

Crissy's green eyes widened. "Jimmy's the
father, isn't he?" She reached across the table
and touched Noelle's arm. "You learned he'd
died what, four weeks ago, and now you're
pregnant? Are you all right? Are you terrified?
I'd be terrified."

Under any other circumstances, the three of
them would never have met and become friends.
Crissy was thirty, the owner of a small chain of
gyms for women. Rachel was twenty-six and a
kindergarten teacher. Noelle was the baby of

the group, but they never made her feel younger or out of place. Right now, with everything going on in her life, Noelle appreciated their support more than she could say.

"I'm still trying to figure out what I feel," Noelle admitted. "Jimmy being gone sort of changes everything."

"You have to tell the family," Rachel said firmly. "They have the right to know a part of Jimmy lives on."

Crissy wrinkled her nose. "But then they'll get involved before Noelle knows what she wants to do. What if she wants to give the baby up for adoption? I mean that makes the most sense." She turned to Noelle. "You're still in college. There are so many deserving couples out there who would be fabulous parents."

Rachel shook her head. "She's not going to do that. Besides, the family has a right to know." She looked at Noelle. "Didn't you say Jimmy has a brother?"

"Yes. Devlin Hunter."

"There you go," Rachel said. "Maybe he wants to be a part of his late brother's child's life."

"So some guy is going to raise Noelle's baby?" Crissy asked. "I don't think so."

"I never thought of adoption," Noelle admitted. There hadn't been time. One second she'd seen the writing on the stick and the next, Dev knew, too. "But it's not an issue. Jimmy's brother knows about the baby and he wants us to get married. I wasn't sure I would agree at first, but now I do. So we're engaged."

She thought about the diamond ring tucked in the back of her lingerie draw. Should she have brought it to show them? Should she—

She realized both women were staring at her as if she'd suddenly morphed into a zebra. She'd thought the baby announcement had been shocking enough, but apparently this one was worse. Their eyes were wide, their mouths open.

Crissy recovered first. "Maybe you should start at the beginning," she said.

Noelle explained about taking the test in Dev's

office and what had happened afterward. She left out the part about her parents being in debt. That wasn't something she wanted to share.

She talked about how Dev had reacted and his proposal. As she told the story, she still found it difficult to believe this was happening.

"Are you insane?" Crissy asked, then winced. "Sorry. I didn't mean that to come out so harshly. But are you insane?"

Rachel shook her head. "In a way, it makes sense. Dev is doing what his brother would have done." She frowned. "Jimmy would have married you, right?"

"He said he wanted to," Noelle said, although she wasn't completely sure he would have come through.

"So it's just one brother stepping in for the other," Rachel said. "It could happen."

"Not in my neighborhood," Crissy said. "Weren't you in love with Jimmy? How can you marry his brother?"

"It's a marriage of convenience," Rachel said.

"All the rules are spelled out. This isn't about being in love. It's about doing the right thing. Dev wants to take care of Noelle and the baby. I think that's great. They'll always be family and be connected. Family is everything."

As her friends continued to argue the point, Noelle realized she hadn't thought of the fact that she and Dev would always be in each other's lives in one way or another. The baby would bind them together the way children always bound parents together.

Parents. She had trouble thinking of herself that way, although for Dev, it was a familiar role. He'd raised Jimmy for years. Knowing he would know what he was doing made her feel better about marrying him.

He'd been great about everything. Kind and generous and patient. Okay, and gorgeous. Under other circumstances…

She mentally put on the brakes. What was she thinking? Dev wasn't interested in anything but a business deal. Besides, what about Jimmy?

Had they been in love? She honestly didn't know. She'd felt more strongly about him than she had about any other guy she'd dated. She'd cried when she'd heard he died and had missed him. But love? What did love feel like? How could anyone be sure?

Crissy smiled at her. "We just want you to be happy. And look at the bright side—no more first dates for a long time. That's thrilling."

Rachel nodded her agreement. "Is this what you want?"

Noelle thought about Dev and how he was willing to be there for her and the baby. How she would now be able to protect her parents from more financial burden and still pursue her nursing degree.

"I wouldn't have chosen to get pregnant," she admitted. "But if I had to then I'm glad Dev is willing to marry me and give the baby a name."

"Then 'yay' Dev," Rachel said. "Wouldn't you know that the youngest of the group is the first to get married."

Crissy looked at her. "Do you want to be married? You've never said anything."

Rachel shrugged. "I wouldn't mind a family of my own. I've always thought about that. What about you?"

Crissy shook her head. "I don't get the whole kid thing. And giving birth? Way too many fluids."

"I agree with the fluids," Rachel said with a grin. "But what about a man to come home to?"

"That would require dating," Crissy told her. "I don't date. Especially first dates. They're the worst. Besides, I have a cat. He's more than enough. I have friends and a great life."

Noelle laughed. "What about a really cute guy?"

"He's a really cute cat. Seriously, I'm fine being single. I never had that burning need to bond with someone."

Noelle wondered why. Didn't everyone have a biological need to connect? She knew she'd always imagined herself getting married and having a family. Funny how now she was doing both, and neither felt especially real.

* * *

"Thanks for agreeing to go from the office," Noelle said. "I know you offered to go from my house, but I haven't told my parents about you yet and…"

Her voice trailed off.

Dev glanced at her, then returned his attention to the road as he drove to the restaurant. "We were both at work. It's fine."

She was obviously nervous and he was willing to admit the situation was unusual.

"You're being really nice about everything," she said. "I'll get better at this, I promise. I just need a little time."

"We both need that," he said, knowing it was true. "That's why we're having dinner—so we can work out the logistics. Decide when I'm going to meet your parents and what we're going to say to them."

She nodded.

She was sensible, he thought. He'd been watching her in the office and she seemed good at her job. Katherine said she was well-liked. Together, he thought, wondering what she'd seen in his brother.

On the heels of that came guilt. Guilt over what had happened to Jimmy and guilt for taking what his brother had lost—his girl and his baby. Something Jimmy—were he alive— wouldn't understand. Of course, if Jimmy were alive, none of this would be an issue.

Dev reminded himself he didn't want Noelle, he was simply doing the right thing. Still, he felt regret and wished Jimmy were here to be the one to marry her.

At the restaurant, he handed the keys to the valet and then walked around the car, put his hand on Noelle's back and guided her into the restaurant. Once there, he gave his name to the hostess and they were shown to a quiet table in the corner.

"This place is very nice," Noelle said with a smile as she was seated with her back to the main dining area. "I've heard about it, of course, but I've never eaten here." She wrinkled her nose. "We don't eat out that much and with my friends, we do more lunch kind of stuff."

She accepted the menu the waiter offered. Dev reached out for his, but realized the young man wasn't paying attention to him at all. Instead he seemed mesmerized by Noelle. It was only when the server had left that Dev looked at her, really looked, and saw her as others would. As a young woman rather than just the girl who had dated his brother.

She was pretty, he thought with some surprise. Her skin was smooth and pale, her eyes a dark blue. Long blond hair hung well past her shoulders. Her dress hugged full curves although he remembered a narrow waist and hips.

Her body got his attention and *his* body responded automatically. The sudden arousal and heat stunned him. What the hell? There was no way anything was going to happen between them. She was pregnant and his brother's girl. What was wrong with him?

He focused on the menu and pushed all other thoughts from his mind, although a lingering heat remained. Noelle was nothing but someone in need. She was going to be like a sister to him. A much younger sister. There could never be anything between them.

Unfortunately his promise to keep his vows popped into his head just then and he mentally groaned at the thought of two years of celibacy. Two very long years. Yet the thought of cheating wasn't appealing, either.

"Everything looks great," Noelle said as she read the menu. "Are there any dishes you recommend?"

They talked about the menu until they ordered, then Dev leaned back in his chair. "I have some paperwork I want you to look over," he told her. "My lawyer wrote up an agreement. It's very straightforward and there aren't any surprises. The details are as we discussed. The baby will have Hunter as his or her last name. There will be a trust set up for the child, along with child support and a monthly income for you. When we divorce, you will be able to buy a house. With real estate values going up so much, I didn't set a specific value. Instead, I've specified the type and size."

The waiter arrived with their drinks. Dev picked up his. "Your copy is in the car, along with a list of lawyers who are familiar with this kind of agreement and a letter saying I'll pay for the consultation." He leaned forward. "I'm serious about this, Noelle. Don't take my word for what I'm telling you. Have someone knowledgeable look the document over and give you an opinion."

The more he insisted on her getting her own legal advice, the more she felt she didn't need it, Noelle thought. But she would do as he asked. It was smart and he was making it easy.

"I know you're not trying to cheat me," she said. "I'm not concerned."

"You have no reason to trust me."

That made her smile. "Dev, when you found

out I was pregnant with your brother's child, the first thing you did was propose. You never asked for a test to prove the baby was Jimmy's, you didn't accuse me of trying to trap him or you. I appreciate all that. You're the kind of man who does the right thing. I respect your principles."

He stiffened and she wondered what she'd said that was wrong. Before she could ask what, he said, "We need to discuss the wedding. I think sooner is better than later."

As much as she didn't want to admit it, he was right. It wasn't as if she were getting any less pregnant by the day.

"Las Vegas is an option," he continued. "It's close and easy. Most of the hotels there will be happy to arrange the wedding. We could fly out on a Saturday morning and be back by midday Sunday."

"That's fast," she murmured.

Las Vegas. She had an immediate picture of a tacky chapel and an Elvis impersonator performing the ceremony. A far cry from the large, elegant affair she'd always pictured for herself. She imagined her sisters as her bridesmaids and her father giving her away.

Dev surprised her by reaching across the table and touching her hand. "You'll have your dream wedding next time," he said.

How had he known what she was thinking? "Las Vegas is fine. It makes the most sense."

His dark gaze settled on her face. "I thought we'd wait until we'd been married a few weeks before telling your family about the baby."

She nodded slowly, liking the warmth of his fingers on hers. "That's for the best. The wedding will be enough for them to take in at first."

She didn't want to think about how everyone would react. Her mother would be hurt to be excluded from such an important event and her father…her father would want to be sure she really loved Dev.

She didn't know how she was going to get around that question, so she would have to do her best to avoid it.

So much to think about, she thought as their salads arrived. So much change so quickly.

"I thought it would be less complicated to tell your parents after the fact about the wedding," he said. "When we get back, we can drive over and tell them it's done. Then you'll move into the house."

Noelle put down her fork and stared at him. Of course she'd known that getting married meant living in the same house, but she hadn't thought through the reality of moving into Dev's home or moving out of her own.

"There are two guestrooms joined by a bathroom," he continued. "That should work for you and the baby. I have a cleaning service that comes in once a week."

She knew people hired them, but she didn't know anyone who did. "I can clean the house," she told him.

He smiled. "You don't have to. The house is big, plus there's the pool house. Besides, you'll be busy with college and the baby. Your education is important, Noelle. I know getting pregnant screwed up your plan, but I want to make sure when we get divorced, you're well on your way to achieving all you want."

"I find it hard to talk about getting married and divorced in the same conversation," she admitted. "I saw a couple of my friends yesterday and I'm going to ask you the same question they asked me. Are you crazy?"

"Not that I'm aware of, although I've heard the psychiatric patient is always the last to know. What are you worried about?"

She liked that he didn't dismiss her concerns or try to convince her everything was fine.

"Nothing specific, just this isn't anything I ever thought I'd do. I don't know how I feel anymore. The baby isn't real to me. I haven't had any symptoms. Just what that stick told me."

"Do you think the stick is wrong?"

She shook her head. "No, I'm guessing it's right. We're talking about getting married and I don't even know how old you are."

"Thirty."

Okay. One question down, four thousand left. "What do you expect from me when we're married? You have a cleaning service. Do I greet you at the door and ask you about your day? Have dinner ready? Is our marriage going to be more *Brady Bunch* or *Married with Children*?"

"How about *The Simpsons*? I think you'd look great with blue hair."

She eyed him. The humor surprised her, but in a good way. "You don't look anything like Homer."

"I could try."

"Please don't." Dev was handsome and elegant, in a James Bond sort of way.

"Noelle, we'll make this relationship what we want it to be. I'd like us to be friends first. That's going to take some time. If you want to cook, I won't say no. I'm tired of take-out and frozen dinners. If you aren't interested, that's fine, too. I don't have any rules."

"But I like rules," she told him. "I like things neatly defined."

"An unexpected pregnancy has a way of changing the rules."

She knew he was right. "What about decorating or entertaining?"

"You can change anything in the house except my study. I have the name of the designer I used. You can call her or pick someone else, or do it yourself. As for entertaining..." He hesitated. "Let's get used to being married, first."

"Okay." She drew in a deep breath and tried to relax. "You know, you can change your mind about marrying me."

He shook his head. "I'm committed to this, Noelle. Are you?"

Sometimes she felt she was doing the right thing and others she felt she was flirting with disaster. But she'd made up her mind and given her word and she was going to keep it.

"This is what I want," she said.

"Then Marge and Homer Simpson it is."

* * *

Noelle checked the purchase order against the packing slip, then compared both with the bill from the supplier. Part of her job included random audits on all the departments. The computer would generate a list of purchases or sales every month and she would walk through the entire process to make sure everything was the way it was supposed to be. She then wrote up a report for Katherine, her boss, who passed it along to Dev.

In the past, she'd never much thought about him reading her findings or critiquing them. All her feedback came through Katherine. But now all that was different—at least on her end. Did Dev notice the e-mails that came from her? Did he think of her differently now?

Not that she would ask, she thought humorously. There were already enough awkward conversations without her throwing one more into the mix.

Katherine, a tall blonde in her late fifties,

paused by Noelle's desk. "If you have a minute, could I see you in my office?"

"Sure." Noelle saved her work on the computer and followed her boss down the hallway.

Katherine's office was next to Dev's and while smaller, was still bright and beautifully decorated. The muted colors blended with the dark wood furniture. Had Noelle wanted to stay in business, she thought that Katherine would be the perfect role model. The woman had started out working in shipping and had risen to be second in command to the president of the company. Nothing happened at Hunter Manufacturing without Katherine knowing about it.

Noelle sat on the chair opposite the desk and waited. Katherine smiled at her.

"Dev's gone this afternoon," she began. "I'm telling you that so you won't worry about him interrupting us or hearing our conversation."

Okay, so they weren't going to discuss Noelle's performance. "All right." Then she realized that Katherine and Dev had been working together for years and it was very likely he'd told her about the impending marriage.

Katherine confirmed her guess when she said, "I understand congratulations are in order."

Noelle shifted in her seat. What on earth was she supposed to say? "I know it probably seems fast," she mumbled. What would Katherine think of her?

But her boss's eyes remained kind. "Life has a way of making things interesting. Still, I can't tell you how sorry I am to lose you."

"I'm not excited about quitting, either," Noelle admitted. "But under the circumstances, it seemed best." Being Dev's assistant's secretary would be more than a little awkward once the marriage took place.

Katherine studied her intently. "I knew you were dating Jimmy. He was an interesting young man. Dev put a lot of effort into his brother." She paused. "Jimmy was fun, but not necessarily someone you would want to trust with your future. Dev is a good man. I've known him since he was a teenager. You can trust him, Noelle. I wanted to wish you the best and tell you that I hope you'll consider the possibilities."

Noelle didn't know what to say. Had Katherine guessed some version of the truth? It sounded like it. Noelle was confident Dev wouldn't say anything without telling her first.

"I agree Dev is a good man." That fact made all of this possible.

"He deserves someone to love him. There have been…disappointments in his life."

Disappointments? More than Jimmy's death?

It occurred to Noelle that she knew very little about the man she would be marrying. He took responsibility, he was kind, but who was he really?

Katherine smiled. "I think the two of you will be very happy together."

"Thank you," Noelle murmured and found herself wishing that were possible.

* * *

Under normal circumstances, Dev would consider himself something of a catch. He had a career, owned a successful business and whoever married him would never want for money. He thought of himself as a good person at heart, although there were plenty of flaws. Still, he'd never had a problem attracting or keeping women around.

He'd also never dated a minister's daughter before and wondered what, exactly, Noelle's parents would make of him. He was a few years older, but that could be a plus. They didn't know about the baby, so they wouldn't be expecting a sudden wedding.

As he parked in front of the modest two-story home in the middle of a suburban neighborhood, he reminded himself that he was doing the right thing for the right reason. Somehow he would convince Noelle's parents that they were made for each other.

At least he should have an easier time of it

than Jimmy would have. His little brother had been every parent's nightmare. Wild, hard-living and willing to do anything on a bet. Not a recipe for happiness.

An unexpected pang of loneliness startled him. Damn. He didn't want to miss his brother, but it seemed that he didn't have a choice. Just when he least expected it, he found himself wanting to tell Jimmy something. Like now. His brother would think the entire situation was a badass joke.

Or would he? Maybe Jimmy would resent Dev stepping in for him—taking what should have been his.

As he climbed from the car, Noelle burst out of the front of the house.

"You're here," she said as she approached.

"Did you doubt me?"

"I thought about running away," she said with a smile that didn't erase the fear in her eyes. "I can only imagine what you've been through." She glanced back at the house. "Okay, everyone is here. It's just a barbecue, right? No big deal. My parents are really nice. My sisters will try to torture you, but don't let them. I'm pretty sure I've already told you everything you need to know." She bit her lower lip. "Do you think we can fake them out? I don't know if I can. I've never done anything like this before and I'm afraid I'll throw up."

She was the most honest woman he'd ever known, he thought humorously. No one else he'd ever dated would have confessed any of that—especially the throwing up part.

She looked pretty in a pale summer dress, with her long hair in a loose disarray of curls. Her eyes were dark with apprehension and her mouth trembled.

His gaze settled on her lips, and without thinking, he bent down and kissed her. The light touch was meant only to distract her, although he enjoyed the brief sensation of softness and heat, and wouldn't mind repeating it. Not that he would.

Apparently it worked because confusion and shock replaced the fear.

"You kissed me," she said as if she could barely believe it.

"Is that a problem?"

"What? No. It's good, in case anyone was watching."

"Now breathe and relax. We'll be fine."

Fine? Fine? Noelle could think of a lot of words, but fine wasn't one of them. Devlin Hunter had kissed her. On the lips. And she'd liked it.

Oh, sure, it obviously hadn't been significant, but still. Now he'd taken her hand in his and they were walking toward the house.

The handholding, like the kiss, didn't mean anything. From what she'd seen so far, he was a man who liked to touch. That was good to know because when the baby came he or she was going to need a lot of physical contact. She liked that Dev wouldn't be a standoffish father. The fact that his almost brotherly kiss had caused her brain to shut down was immaterial. And strange.

As they reached the front door, she had the sudden horrifying thought that there was the tiniest possibility that she was attracted to Dev. But she'd been dating Jimmy and was carrying Jimmy's baby. And Dev was only doing this to take responsibility—something he did on a regular basis.

They had a very logical, well-thought-out agreement. There was no way she was going to muddle that by being attracted to him. It wasn't right. It wasn't what she wanted.

Just a fluke, she told herself. Nothing more. And as of this exact moment, it would never happen again.

Chapter Four

Noelle hyperventilated all the way to the front door. She was nervous and scared and still wondering about the kiss. But before she could pick a dominant emotion, they were in the house, and Tiffany, the baby of the family and already annoying at fifteen, yelled, "Noelle's boyfriend is here, Mom."

Dev squeezed her fingers in reassurance. At least that's what she thought it was. That or he was expecting her to bolt and he was doing his best to keep her in place.

Noelle led him through the living room, into the kitchen, where her mother stood chopping vegetables for a salad.

"Mom, this is Devlin Hunter," Noelle said, then swallowed. "Dev, my mother. Jane Stevenson."

"Mrs. Stevenson," Dev said easily and offered her mother his right hand.

Noelle's mother looked up. Her eyes widened slightly in shock, then she smiled and shook hands with him. "Nice to meet you, Dev. Welcome. Please call me Jane. I hope you like chicken and burgers."

"Who doesn't?" he asked easily.

Her mother glanced at Noelle. "Your father is in the yard. Go on and introduce Dev. Then you can come back and help me with the rest of the food."

Noelle nodded and walked Dev through the kitchen and laundry room, then out into the backyard.

Her father stood by a large barbecue. He had on a ridiculous chef's hat and an apron that said in bold green letters, "I'm Irish. Kiss the cook."

"That doesn't apply to you," she murmured in Dev's ear.

"Good to know. I have to draw a line somewhere."

That made her laugh, so for a second she forgot to be terrified as she introduced Dev to her father.

"Daddy, this is Devlin Hunter. Dev, my father, Robert Stevenson."

Dev released her hand and nodded at her father. "Sir."

Her dad raised his eyebrows. "I like the sir part, but Bob is fine. Unless you'd like to call me Sir Bob."

Dev grinned. "Is it important to you?"

"I can live without it."

There was a large shriek from the edge of the pool. Noelle turned and saw eight or ten teenaged girls either in the pool or lying around it.

"My sisters," she said with a sigh. "And some of their friends. I'll bore you with them later."

"Good idea," her father told her. "Don't

frighten him off just yet. Let's lull him into a false sense of security and then we'll let the girls loose." He glanced at Dev. "Want a beer?"

Dev's surprise was obvious. Her father laughed.

"Yes, I can be a pastor and still drink beer."

"Good to know. Whatever you're having."

Her father held up his can.

"I'll get it," Noelle said and hurried back inside the house.

She found her mother still making salad, but as soon as she entered the kitchen, her mother turned on her.

"You said you were dating a guy from work, Noelle. I thought you mean someone stocking shelves or something. He's the president of the company."

Her heart sank. Were they going to be found out so quickly.

"I know, but he's—"

Her mother cut her off with a quick wave of her head. "I'm not complaining. He seems very nice and obviously he's smart. He's also well-off. I'm impressed." Her mother laughed. "Oh, my. I sound like the mother in *Pride and Prejudice,* when she got so excited about someone having an income of four thousand a year."

"He's older," Noelle said tentatively, not sure she was hearing correctly. Did her mother actually *approve?* "There's ten years between us."

"I know. Maybe with one of your sisters I'd worry, but you've always been sensible and mature. I'm sure that comes from being the oldest. He won't bore you like the boys your age." She grinned again, then lowered her voice. "Don't tell your father I said so, but he's very good-looking."

Noelle laughed. "Yes, he is," she said as she looked out the window and saw Dev standing in conversation with her father. "Sexy, even."

"Definitely sexy."

She'd just been saying the words, but as she watched him laugh, she noticed the shape of his mouth and how broad his shoulders were. He wore yet another Hawaiian shirt tucked into khaki shorts, and his lean muscles were clearly displayed.

He *was* good-looking, she thought in surprise as she felt a faint tingle. And funny and charming and smart and pretty much everything she'd ever wanted. But not for her. Their's was a marriage of convenience. She was carrying Jimmy's baby. Having a relationship with his brother was wrong on so many levels. It wasn't to be, she thought wistfully. Not ever.

Despite the large crowd of teenagers, everyone sat down together to eat. Instead of a table, they sprawled on the lawn in the shade of an old tree, even Noelle's parents.

Dev found himself surrounded by her sisters and on the receiving end of some serious grilling.

"How long have you and Noelle been going out?" one of the sisters asked. They were all blond-haired, blue-eyed California types and there was no way he could tell them apart.

"Four months," he said easily, remembering when Jimmy had first gone out with Noelle.

"Do you like how she kisses?" asked the one who was obviously the youngest.

"Tiffany," Jane said in a warning voice to her daughter.

"It's a legitimate question," she said, then sighed. "Fine, what do you like about her? She's bossy. Did she tell you that? She's always getting on me to do my homework or clean up my mess in the bathroom." She inched closer, then spoke in a whisper. "She goes crazy when I leave the sink dirty. Honestly, who really cares about that stuff?"

"I can hear you," her mother said from across the lawn.

Tiffany sighed. "Fine."

Dev glanced up and saw Noelle watching him. He winked at her and was pleased when she blushed and smiled.

"You like own the company, right?" one of the other sisters asked.

"It's been in my family for many years," Dev told her. "I inherited it from my father."

"He's rich," she whispered to the sister sitting next to her. "Cool."

Jane groaned. "Obviously I've failed miserably with these girls. I apologize, Dev."

"No need."

Compared to how he'd screwed up things with Jimmy, she'd been brilliant.

The questions continued, some easy, some more difficult, until the meal was finished. After everyone had tossed their paper plates into the big trash can by the garage, Noelle and her mother went into the kitchen for a couple of minutes, then returned with huge flats of fresh strawberries. Her father stood and faced everyone.

"It's Sunday," he said.

There was a collective groan from Noelle's sisters, although their guests looked more expectant than unhappy. Dev wondered what significance the day of the week held.

Bob glanced at him. "On Sunday, we all talk

about something unexpected that happened in our week and how it has changed us for the better. We'll let you go later so you can see how it's done."

Dev looked at Noelle, who mouthed an apology. From her stricken expression he could tell she felt bad for not warning him about this.

He was sure he could come up with something. Noelle could win the prize for unexpected news, but he doubted she would be sharing information about her pregnancy or their engagement. So what would she say?

Bob cleared his throat. "I'll go first." He glanced at his wife, who—with Noelle—was slicing ripe strawberries into bowls and setting them out on the table.

"Jane came to me and told me she wanted to take a job outside the church office this week. At first I was angry. I thought she was turning her back on our responsibilities to our community." He smiled slightly. "As I thought about the situation more, I realized my anger didn't come from that at all. Jane has never walked away from anything that needed doing. So why was I so upset?"

He paused. "Eventually I realized I was upset because I would miss seeing her all the time. I've spent our marriage with the luxury of always being with the woman I love. I know being apart for a few hours a day is something I can endure, but knowing she won't be there makes me appreciate the time we do have together."

He raised his bottle of water toward his wife.

Jane smiled. "Thank you, honey."

"You're welcome."

Tiffany groaned. "Please do *not* kiss. I beg you. It's gross."

One of her friends bumped her shoulder. "It's not gross, it's romantic. I wish my parents still kissed."

Tiffany made a gagging noise.

Her father looked at her. "Maybe you'd like to go next."

Tiffany sighed heavily, then stood and told

about a book she'd read that had been on her summer reading list that she'd dreaded and how it had turned out to be really good. Now she knew that maybe she should give books a chance before deciding they were stupid.

And so it went. Even the friends of the sisters stood and talked about something unexpected in their day. Some of them spoke eagerly and Dev wondered if this was the only place they got any positive adult attention.

When it was Noelle's turn, he wondered what she would say. She stood and smiled at him.

"My boss called me into her office this week," she began. "I've talked about Katherine before. She's great. I love working for her. Anyway, she knew Dev and I were, ah, dating."

He hoped he was the only one who noticed the hesitation in her voice before she said the "d" word. He'd mentioned the engagement to Katherine, who hadn't acted surprised. He wondered if she'd already figured out the truth.

"She told me that sometimes things happen in different ways than we expected and that we should be open to that. Then she told me that Dev is a good man and that I was lucky to have him in my life."

All eyes shifted to him. He stared at Noelle, intrigued that Katherine had talked to her and that she had chosen that as her story.

"I already knew you were a good man," she said with a smile, "but it was nice to have it confirmed by an outside source."

Everyone laughed.

The next person spoke, but Dev kept his attention on Noelle. There were depths to her he hadn't expected. So far all the discoveries were positive. If they'd met under different circumstances…but they hadn't. Besides, Noelle was the type to believe in happily-ever-after and he thought romantic love was a crock. He'd seen what "love" had done to his mother.

It had killed her.

"Your turn," Bob said a few minutes later.

Dev stood. "Noelle has talked about her family in glowing terms," he said. "Mostly I thought it was just that—talk. But now that I've met you, I see she was modest in her praise. You are a true family and spending the day with you has given me an idea of what I want for my own family someday."

He hadn't planned what he was going to say and it revealed more than he would have liked. Still, it was true. He might not have a lot of faith in the love between a man and a woman but he believed in family. Maybe because his had never been what he wanted.

He saw Bob and Jane exchange a pleased glance, then look at Noelle. Obviously they approved of him for their daughter.

His gut tightened. Until that moment he hadn't considered that doing the right thing meant deceiving two very decent people. What consequences would Noelle have to face later?

Still, there was no going back. Not with Jimmy's child on the line.

* * *

The following weekend Noelle managed to ignore the reason for the plane trip right up until they stepped off the escalator in the massive baggage claim area and she saw a man in a suit holding a sign that said "Hunter."

Then reality crashed in and she realized that she was hours away from being Mrs. Hunter.

Married. Was it possible? The need to scream built up inside of her, but before she could decide if she would give in or not, Dev walked over to the man.

"That's us," he said, motioning to the sign.

"Mr. Hunter," the man said with a smile. "I'm Johnson. Do you have any luggage."

Dev indicated the small wheeled bags they'd carried onto the plane. "This is it."

"Very good, sir."

Johnson took her bag and led the way to a large white limo. While the luggage was stowed, Dev opened the rear door and motioned for Noelle to climb in first.

She'd only been in one other limo. That had been a little over a year ago for her senior prom. She'd squeezed in with four other couples and had laughed the entire way to the hotel where the dance had been held. However she didn't think that was something she should share with Dev.

Instead she sat on the pale leather seat and did her best to keep from passing out.

He glanced at her, then reached for her hand. "Breathe."

"You tell me that a lot," she murmured, once again aware of the warmth of his fingers against hers and how being close to him made her feel safe.

"You've been panicked a lot lately. We're fine. We'll get through this and then the worst will be over."

She wasn't sure about that. "I've never done anything like this before."

He grinned. "Run off and get married? It's a first for me, too."

She smiled back at him. "It's not just the running off. It's everything else."

"Piece of cake," he told her. "Pretend it's just a regular weekend. We're here to have fun."

"Regular weekend?" she asked with squeak. "We barely know each other and we're getting married because I'm pregnant with your late brother's child. I don't know what you do for fun, but I tend to avoid situations like this."

He leaned in and kissed her forehead. "You'll be fine."

She wanted to believe him, but wasn't sure she could. She kept a hold of his hand and studied the sights as they drove from the airport to the Vegas Strip.

Traffic was slow and it took a long time to get down to the Bellagio. Noelle recognized the beautiful lake in front of the massive hotel from scenes in television and the movies.

"I've never been here," she murmured.

"At the Bellagio or in Las Vegas?"

"Both."

"I think you'll like it."

The limo pulled around to the main entrance. A uniformed man opened the rear door and Dev stepped out. He waited for her to join him, gave his name to the bellman, tipped the driver, then led her inside.

The first thing she noticed was a beautiful art glass ceiling. Everywhere she looked she saw glass flowers in a rainbow of colors. The detail was incredible, as was the sheer mass of flowers. From there Dev led her to a conservatory decorated in celebration of the upcoming Fourth of July holiday.

Paths crisscrossed between gardens and clever displays of flowers and patriotic arrangements.

"I love it!" she said with a grin. "This is amazing."

"They know how to impress," he said. "Come on."

He led her through part of the casino. Gaming tables stretched out for what looked like miles.

There were tons of slot machines and a level of noise that surprised her.

"So many people are gambling," she said. "Where do they get the money?"

"It's entertainment. Plus, everyone is hoping to get lucky and hit the big one."

She'd brought ten dollars to gamble with. Somehow that didn't seem enough to hit the big one.

They made their way to the VIP check-in. Dev offered a credit card and signed a form. While the uniformed man was processing their keys, Dev turned to her.

"I meant to give this to you before we left," he said.

He handed her a credit card. She glanced down and saw it was in her name.

"Unless you buy an expensive car," he said, "You can't reach the spending limit. Use it however you want."

The clerk handed over a small folder containing their room keys and gave instructions to the elevator.

"I don't need this," she whispered as they walked away from registration.

"Yes, you do," he told her. "How are you going to buy groceries or get gas or pick up things for the house? What if you want clothes or shoes or a puppy?"

She blinked at him. "I couldn't really handle a puppy right now."

"I know." He took her hand. "Noelle, we're getting married. A credit card comes with the ring."

She wasn't sure she could ever be comfortable spending his money, but if she weren't working it wasn't as if she were going to be supporting herself.

"I don't think I like this part," she said in a low voice.

"Didn't you read the paperwork? I promised to support you for the length of our marriage."

"Reading it and living it are very different."

He pushed the Up button for the elevator. "Hadn't you planned on being a stay-at-home mother?"

"Eventually," she admitted. "I'd thought I'd go back to work when the kids were in school, but for the first few years..." Her voice trailed off as she saw him looking at her. She sighed. "This is different."

"No. It's not."

They stepped into the elevator.

"While we're at the hotel, you can charge anything you'd like to the room," he said. "Just give them the room number and your name. We're both listed."

While she pondered that, they arrived on their floor. She hadn't paid attention to their room number, so she didn't know which way to turn. Fortunately, he kept hold of her hand and she simply followed him down a lovely hallway.

Their hotel room had double doors. Dev opened the one on the right and she stepped into a massive sitting room that was probably the size of the whole downstairs of her parents' house.

There was a round table big enough for six, a wet bar, two sitting areas and a television nearly as big as a movie screen.

"We'll have to discover it all ourselves," Dev said, putting down the keys on a marble entry table. "Usually the manager comes up and explains all the amenities, but I wasn't sure you could take one more thing."

She tried to smile in gratitude, but she was too shocked by everything. Who on earth would get a room like this and how much could it cost?

He crossed the room and pulled the sheers aside. "Come look."

She moved next to him and saw they had a view of the lake, along with several of the hotels around them.

"We'll be able to see the water show," he said. "You'll enjoy that. Come on."

He led her across the sitting room and into the biggest bedroom she'd ever seen. There was a bed that could easily sleep five, a small sofa, a desk, floor-to-ceiling windows and carpeting so plush she nearly sank to her ankles. All of which was lovely, but then she saw both their suitcases on a bench at the foot of the bed and her throat tightened.

Were they sharing? Logically the bed was plenty big enough. And once they were married, it wasn't as if she could refuse Dev. He would be her husband. Marriage of convenience or not, if he had expectations, she wasn't sure she could in good conscience say no.

She could ask for time, though, right? That was reasonable. He would have to understand that under the circumstances she couldn't be expected to—

He stepped in front of her, cupped her face in his hands and said, "Stop. Whatever you're thinking, just stop."

She stared at him. "How did you know?"

"The sudden look of panic on your face." He dropped his hands. "Noelle, I meant what I said.

We're doing this for the baby. I'm not trying to seduce you. I know they left both our suitcases here, but the suite has a second bedroom where I'll be sleeping."

Relief made her knees nearly give way. "Really?"

He smiled. "I promise. Look, as we just discussed, neither of us has been married before. This is going to be a big change. We'll take it slow, okay?"

She nodded.

He touched her chin. "Hey, I've never even lived with a woman before."

Really? She found the thought comforting. "But you've gone away for weekends with them," she said.

He shrugged. "Once or twice."

She smiled. "More than that. You have a reputation, Mr. Hunter."

"Really. And what would that be?"

"That you have had a string of incredibly beautiful, exotic women in your life."

"Huh. I never knew anyone was paying attention."

"They were."

She stared into his amused eyes and felt some of her fear ease. Maybe this was the strangest situation she'd ever been in, but they were in it together and somehow that made things easier.

He stepped back. "We have a couple of hours until the wedding. Are you hungry?"

When he said the "w" word, all her fears and worries crashed into her. She nearly staggered from the impact.

"I can't eat," she told him, her stomach getting upset just at the thought of food.

"Okay. Why don't you rest? We need to leave here about three-thirty."

She glanced at her watch. "I'll be ready."

"Good." He walked to the door, then glanced back at her. "You can still change your mind."

She shook her head. "I want to do this," she said, hoping she sounded confident and sure, instead of terrified. "I'll be ready."

* * *

Despite not having slept in nearly three nights, resting was impossible, so Noelle alternatively paced the length of the beautiful bedroom and stared out at the incredible view. An hour before it was time to go, she plugged in her electric curlers, then checked her dress for wrinkles.

After curling her hair, she redid her makeup, then changed into a strapless bra. She'd found her dress at the outlet mall. It had been one of those great moments in shopping history—with the price marked down four different times and the dress landing under a "50 percent off on this rack only" sign.

The dress was white, with spaghetti straps and an asymmetrical hem. The top was fitted, the skirt full and there were tiny clear crystals angling across fabric.

She supposed it had been a prom dress that hadn't found a home and while it wasn't the dress she'd always imagined for her wedding, she felt pretty when she slipped it on and closed the side zipper.

After she finger-combed the curls and sprayed them until they practically crackled, she reached for the engagement ring she hadn't worn since the night Dev had bought it for her. She hesitated, then slid it on her right hand. When the ceremony was over, she would put it on her left, in front of her wedding band.

Which, she suddenly thought, hadn't been discussed.

Just then Dev knocked on the bedroom door. She crossed the cushy carpet, her high-heel sandals sinking in with each step.

"Hi," she said as she opened the door. "I'm ready."

He looked good in his tailored black suit. Very elegant and in charge.

He smiled. "You're beautiful."

"Thank you." She clutched the tiny white satin evening bag she'd borrowed from Crissy. "Did you, um, think to get wedding bands?"

He patted his jacket pocket. "I have them right here. I picked out platinum, to match your engagement ring."

Before she could say anything, he held out a small bouquet of white roses and starburst lilies.

"For the bride," he told her.

She hadn't expected flowers. Funny how they got to her more than the suite or the expensive engagement ring. Her eyes burned with unshed tears and she willed herself not to cry. Dev had been nothing but sweet and thoughtful. He didn't deserve tears.

She thanked him and they walked to the elevator. The ride down passed with a blur. Suddenly they were in a small chapel and she was reciting that she would love and cherish Dev as long as they both shall live. She hesitated slightly before her "I do" knowing she was making a vow she had every intention of breaking. Then she whispered the words and it was over.

She was aware of someone taking their picture,

then polite conversation with the officiate, followed by a quick ride back up to the room.

"Are you all right?" Dev asked as he inserted the key, then pushed opened the door.

"I'm fine."

She didn't feel any different than she had a half hour ago. Except for the slender platinum band nestled against her engagement ring, there wasn't any proof that anything had changed. Yet she was now married. How was that possible? Shouldn't she feel profoundly transformed?

"Did you eat last night?" he asked.

She turned her attention from her rings to the man she'd married. "What?"

"Let me rephrase that. When was the last time you ate?"

Food, like sleep, hadn't seemed possible. "Thursday."

"That can't be good."

He took her hand and led her toward the large dining table. It was only then she noticed the covered dishes, along with a bottle of champagne chilling in an ice bucket.

"I had a feeling you wouldn't have eaten much," he said. "So I ordered us an early dinner."

He walked to the champagne and expertly popped the cork. After pouring some in two glasses, he handed her one. "I know you're pregnant and only nineteen, but I thought you might want a sip on your wedding day."

She stared at the bubbles rising in the narrow glass, then smiled at him. "Actually, I'm twenty. My birthday was last week."

He frowned. "I'm sorry. I didn't realize I missed it."

Some of her tension eased as she laughed. "I really didn't expect you to notice, Dev. It's not a big deal."

Had they been a real couple, she would have been hurt, but under the circumstances…not so much.

He raised his glass. "To your birthday, a few days late. And to us."

She touched her glass to his, then took a sip.

While the bubbles tickled her tongue, the liquid had no taste. She didn't think it was the champagne's fault, either. At that moment, she doubted she could have tasted anything. She put down her glass and tried to ignore the trembling in her body. She was so tired, she thought. Tired and confused and not sure what he expected of her.

Noelle swayed slightly on her feet. Dev grabbed her arm.

"Are you all right?" he asked, wondering what the hell he would do if she collapsed.

"I'm okay. I haven't been sleeping."

Exhaustion darkened her eyes. Her skin was so pale, it was practically white.

"You want to go lie down?" he asked.

"I won't sleep."

"You might surprise yourself." He spun her toward her room and gave her a push. "Go on."

She turned back to him. "What about the dinner? You went to so much trouble."

"Don't worry about it."

She bit her bottom lip as if not sure if she could do what she wanted instead of what she should. Then she raised herself on tiptoe, whispered, "Thank you," and kissed him on the cheek.

Her lips lingered for half a second and in that moment he was stunned to find himself wanting to turn so that his mouth brushed hers. Only he wanted more than just a simple kiss. He wanted to claim her in a moment of passion that rocked them both.

The need shocked him into stepping back, although he was careful to keep his face expressionless. He gave her another little push and this time she walked into her bedroom and shut the door.

He stood alone in the center of the living room, with an open bottle of champagne and a romantic dinner for two. Ignoring both, he walked to the minibar and pulled out every container of Scotch.

Hell of a way to spend a wedding night, he thought as he opened the first bottle and swallowed the contents.

Chapter Five

Noelle twisted her new rings round and round on her finger. "I keep thinking I've reached the peak stomach-churning experience," she said. "But then a new one crops up. Do you think we're close to done?"

As she spoke, she glanced at Dev, who sat behind the wheel of the car and negotiated the streets that led to her parents' house.

"Once we're through with this, it should be easy," he said.

"Except I have to tell them I'm pregnant."

"Not for a few more weeks."

"I know. I'll try not to think about it."

She was getting good at that—clearing her mind and living in the moment. After the wedding, she'd stretched out on the big bed, thinking she would never sleep. When next she'd surfaced, it had been after midnight and she'd still been in her white dress. She'd showered, washed off her makeup, then crawled into bed where she'd zonked out until nearly eight.

They'd shared a quiet breakfast in one of the cafes, then had flown home at noon. Now they were going by to tell her family the news and pick up several suitcases and return to his house.

Easy enough, as long as she didn't actually think about doing any of it.

Before she'd figured out exactly what she was going to say to her parents, Dev pulled up in front of the house. Noelle got out, then smoothed the front of her cotton skirt and forced herself to smile as she led the way to the door.

"Hi, Mom," she yelled as she entered.

Unlike the previous weekend, this time the house was quiet. All of her sisters were off with friends. But Noelle had called ahead and knew her parents were home.

"Hi, honey," her mom said, stepping out of the kitchen. "Are you hungry? Did you want me to—" She spotted Dev. "Oh, hello. I didn't know you were with Noelle today." She smiled, then yelled. "Bob, Noelle and Dev are here." She looked back at them. "Your father's in his study. He preached from Romans today and you know how he gets."

Noelle turned to Dev. "He goes over his sermons after he gives them and looks at ways he could have done things better."

Her father walked down the hall toward them. "We didn't expect to see you until later." He held out his hand to Dev. "Good to see you again."

"Thank you, sir."

Dev glanced at her, which she knew was her cue. Noelle drew in a deep breath.

"Mom, Dad, I didn't spend the night at Crissy's last night. Dev and I flew to Las Vegas and got married."

Both her parents stared at her in open-mouthed shock. She cleared her throat, then added, "I'm sorry I lied."

Dev stepped into the uncomfortable silence. "It was all my idea," he said quickly. "Please don't blame your daughter. I was doing my best to sweep her off her feet and all the time she kept talking about how she didn't want to disappoint you. I hope you'll understand and lay the blame where it belongs."

Noelle appreciated the support and the fact that Dev wasn't technically lying about anything.

Her mother surfaced first. "Married?" she asked in a shaky voice. "One of my babies is married?"

Noelle held out the ring. Her mother glanced at it, then at Dev. "Okay, yeah, for that I might have married you, too." She gave a laugh, then pulled Noelle close. "Is this what you want? Are you happy?"

Noelle was grateful that the tight hug meant her only response could be a nod.

Her father glared at Dev. "You're sure about this? You're prepared to take on the responsibility for my daughter?"

"Of course," Dev said confidently. "Mr. Stevenson, I know how much your daughter means to you. I would never hurt her in any way. She will be taken care of and safe for as long as I draw breath."

Noelle waited for her father's response. Once again Dev had managed to speak the truth. She wondered if anyone would notice that he hadn't promised to love her.

Her father continued to study Dev for a few more seconds, then held out his hand again. "Then welcome to the family."

"Thank you, sir."

The next few minutes passed in a blur. Her parents ushered them into the family room. Her mother produced lemonade and cookies, then wished they had champagne in the house.

"I didn't think we'd need it so soon," she said, touching Noelle's hand. "Tell me everything about the wedding. I wish we could have been there. Oh, my. There are so many people to tell. We'll have to have a party, won't we, Bob? Maybe something in the garden."

Dev listened to Jane Stevenson talk about the wedding. There were tears in her eyes as she realized all she'd missed of her oldest daughter's big day. He felt bad for having to deceive her and her husband, but it was better this way. Better that they not know the truth about the baby. They were the sort of people who would insist on helping and he didn't want to have to argue against their pride and love for their daughter.

Noelle was holding up better than he'd expected. She answered lots of questions about the Bellagio and even surprised him by admitting she'd already packed most of her things.

When they were finally ready to leave, he braced himself for a one-on-one with Noelle's father. He figured he owed the man, so he wouldn't try to duck out of the conversation. But instead it was Jane who cornered him as Noelle's father loaded her luggage in the car.

"Please take care of my little girl," she said, tears filling her eyes. "I know she's the oldest, but I still think of her as my baby. My firstborn. Oh, Dev, I know you're a good man, but this is difficult."

He touched her arm. "I promise I'll take care of her."

She smiled through her tears. "I know she'll never want for anything, which is lovely, but there's so much more to a marriage than not worrying about bills. Noelle is special. I guess I don't have to tell you that, but I'm going to, anyway. She's smart and responsible and caring. And that's what I worry about the most. Her heart."

She paused and wiped away the single tear that had escaped. "She thinks she's tough, but she bruises so easily. She leads with her heart. Be careful of that. Be tender."

"I will," he said, knowing it was a safe promise. Noelle's heart didn't enter into their agreement.

"As long as you love each other fully, you can get through anything," Jane said. "That's my best advice. Love each other."

He nodded without speaking, then walked toward the car.

Love. Romantic love. He didn't believe in it. Not anymore. He'd tried it once, while he'd been raising Jimmy, only the woman in question had refused to deal with a difficult teenager. He'd let her walk away because he hadn't known how to keep her. The loss had devastated him.

Since then, he'd avoided the emotion and found he got along quite fine. Love was for the weak. He'd always been strong. Nothing about that was going to change.

Since Dev was able to carry about five times as much luggage as Noelle, they carried everything inside in two trips.

"I told you about the two bedrooms down here," he said as he showed her a large, airy bedroom decorated in pale blue and beige. A queen-size bed sat against one wall, with a big armoire opposite. A long desk filled the space under the window.

"I ordered the desk last week and had it put here," he said. "I thought you might like to look out while you studied."

He'd done that for her? "Thank you," she said as she glanced out at the beautiful yard. She could see flowers, a tree and one end of the pool. Talk about a great way to take a break. "It was very thoughtful."

"You're welcome. Bookcases," he said, pointing to the ends of the desk.

She bent down and saw there was a good-sized bookcase at each end. On both sides of the comfy looking leather chair were deep file drawers.

The closet was equally impressive. A big walk-in had been finished by some expert who had put in angled shelves for shoes, straight shelves for folded items, pockets for purses, three sets of drawers and plenty of multilevel hanging space. The fixtures were a gleaming silver that looked great against the light wood.

She walked into the bathroom. There were two sinks and lots more storage space. The far door led into another nice bedroom with a queen-size bed and simple furniture.

"You'll want to make changes," he said. "To make this into a baby's room. I'll give you the name of my decorator. If you'd rather design it yourself, I have a handyman who will move furniture, paint, hang curtains, whatever. All that information is in my study."

He left, apparently wanting to give her that stuff now. Noelle lingered for a second. A baby's room. She tried to imagine the space filled with a crib and changing table, but nothing about this situation seemed real.

She found Dev in his study. He offered her a list of phone numbers, including his personal cell, work cell, private line, the decorator and anyone else he thought she might want to get in touch with.

There was also a leather box filled with an assortment of items. He went through them quickly.

"ATM card, checkbook. Extra key to my car. House key, alarm code. Everything is marked."

"You've been busy," she said, feeling her head start to spin. "All I had to do was pack up a few clothes."

"This is your home now, Noelle."

Was it? Technically, but she didn't think she would feel totally comfortable in the beautiful space for a long time.

"So you're saying I can put my feet up on the coffee table?" she asked.

"You can take a hammer to it, if you'd like."

She winced. "Not my style, although I appreciate the offer."

They smiled at each other. Okay, sure, this was weird and awkward, but Dev was doing his best to make things pleasant and easy. He'd been nothing but thoughtful from the moment he'd found out about the baby.

"You're a really good guy," she said. "Why aren't you married?"

He grinned. "Actually, I am, Mrs. Hunter."

"What? Oh. Me."

"Forgotten already?"

She glanced down at her ring. Mrs. Hunter. Was that her? "Sort of."

He put a hand on her shoulder. "You'll get used to it."

She nodded and started to say something, but the words got lost as she realized how much she wanted to step closer to him. Right now she could do with a good hug and one specifically from Dev. She wanted him to hold her next to him and tell her everything was going to be all right. She wanted to borrow strength from him and listen to his heartbeat and maybe have him…

What? What did she want? She swallowed as the truth uncoiled inside of her.

She wanted him to kiss her.

The thought was so unexpected, she actually took a step back. Kissing? There was no kissing in their relationship. Oh, sure. Slight, friendship-style kisses on the cheek. But not mouth to mouth, breath mingling, tongues touching, I-want-to-melt-into-you kissing. That was not allowed.

"You all right?" he asked.

"Fine," she said in a squeak, then cleared her throat. "Thanks for all of this." She motioned to the box. "I'll, um, try not to go wild at the sales."

"I'm not worried." He hesitated, then said, "There's something else you need to see. Under the circumstances…" He seemed at a loss for words, which was so not Dev. "Jimmy lived here, in the pool house. I'm having it redone into a game room, but before the workmen show up, I thought you might want to look around and see if there's anything you'd like to keep for yourself or the baby. I've already taken a few things for myself."

Jimmy. She hadn't thought about him in days. He was the reason all this had happened and yet he'd practically vanished from her mind.

Guilt battled with her more practical nature. If she'd let him go so easily, apparently what she had felt wasn't love. So what did love feel like and how would she know when it was real?

"If this is a bad time," he began.

"No, it's fine. I appreciate the offer."

She followed him outside. The pool house was a big open room with full bath at one end. A sofa sat in front of a large television. A bed had been pushed against the far wall.

Noelle looked at the sports posters on the walls and a few trophies on a shelf. She waited for a flood of emotion, but there wasn't one. Just sadness for a young man who had died too early.

Several small model cars sat on a window sill. When she crossed to them, Dev said, "He always loved cars. By the time he was ten, he knew more about them than me."

She picked up two cars, then fingered an Angels baseball cap before adding it to her collection. There weren't any personal pictures and she didn't think what looked like a year's worth of *Car and Driver* would be considered significant. Then she spotted the yearbooks.

"You don't want these for yourself?" she asked.

Dev shook his head.

She flipped through one and saw dozens of messages from friends. "I'll keep these, too," she said. "What people write often gives insight into a person. Jimmy's son or daughter might like that."

"Okay. I have a lot of pictures I was going to sort through. Once I figure out when they were taken, I'll put them in order."

"That would be nice."

They returned to the house.

"I thought we'd order dinner in tonight," he said. "Give you a chance to settle in."

She nodded. "I'll go to the grocery store tomorrow and cook dinner. Any requests?"

"You don't have to cook."

"I actually like cooking." She put the items from Jimmy's room on the kitchen counter. "My mom made sure we all knew what we were doing. I don't get very fancy, but everything is eatable."

"Then you pick. I can't remember my last home-cooked meal, so I won't be fussy."

Interesting, she thought. So the slinky, exotic women didn't cook. No doubt they had other talents.

"What time do you usually get home?"

"About six."

"Then I'll plan dinner for six-thirty."

This was so strange—having this very domestic conversation with the man who had been, until recently, her boss.

"I'll leave you to unpack, then," he said. "Let me know if you need any help."

"I will. Thanks."

Dev retreated to his den. He had to find this as strange as she did. They were both being so polite. Would it get easier with time? Would they ever feel comfortable together?

Once again she thought that this was not the marriage she'd always imagined. However, it *was* the one she had. Instead of focusing on what she wanted to be different, maybe it was time to think about how lucky she was to be married to Dev and do what she could to make their two years together fun for both of them.

Noelle had decided on what her mother claimed was every man's favorite—meatloaf and mashed potatoes—for her first home-cooked meal. She wasn't sure of Dev's vegetable preference, so she did a medley, along with a salad. There was strawberry shortcake for dessert and an assortment of ice-cream flavors in the freezer, in case he didn't like the shortcake.

She'd shopped early, then had spent the rest of the morning getting to know Dev's neighborhood and finding things like the closest dry cleaner and drugstore. After that, she'd been on her own. Alone. Completely alone.

She wasn't used to having a house to herself. At her parents' house, there was always someone around. But here…not so much.

She found herself waiting for Dev's arrival with an eagerness that had a lot to do with finally having someone to talk to, but when he walked through the door to the garage, she wasn't sure what to say.

Her parents usually came home together. On the rare nights they didn't, her mother hugged and kissed her father. But that didn't seem right. Smiling at Dev and asking about his day felt weird, as if she were in some play somewhere.

"Dinner will be ready in about ten minutes," she said. "Do you usually change into something casual?" She motioned to his suit. "I mean, you have time. Or I can hold dinner."

"I'll change later." He put his briefcase on the floor, leaning against the end of the cabinets and loosened his tie. "Settling in?"

She nodded. He looked good, she thought as he slipped off his jacket, then went to work, rolling up his shirtsleeves. A little wrinkled, but still handsome. She liked the way his stubble shaded his cheeks and jaw.

"I've found most of the necessities of life."

"How are you feeling?" he asked, his gaze intense.

Feeling? What would she be… Oh. "You mean the baby." She touched her stomach. "Honestly, I don't feel anything. I don't know when I'm supposed to start having symptoms and it's not like I want to ask my mom. I did make a doctor's appointment for a prenatal checkup."

"Good. When is it?"

She told him.

"I'll go with you," he said. "We're in this together, so I'm interested in information, too."

Going with her? "You don't have to."

He smiled. "I want to be there through all of this."

His words gave her a warm kind of glow in her tummy. "Okay. That would be nice. I'll admit I was a little scared. Just because I've never done this before."

"Me, either."

She served dinner and they sat at the round table. Dev told her about what had happened at the office that day. When he was finished, she said, "I've signed up for summer school. I'm taking calculus." She wrinkled her nose. "Math is not my thing, but it's required, so I decided to get it out of the way in one intense, horrible six-week period. I go for three hours a day, four days a week. I start Monday."

"That's a lot of calculus."

"I know. I don't want to think about the homework, but I keep telling myself by the middle of August, it will be over."

"This is excellent," he said, cutting off another piece of meatloaf. "I'm now officially won over by your cooking, but don't worry if you don't have time once you're in school. Getting your education should be your priority."

"And the baby."

"The baby won't arrive until next year."

She nodded. "I guess I'll be due in early March."

"So you can go to the fall semester and then

take the spring semester off. And graduate the following January."

She hadn't thought that far ahead. "I like that. The baby will be what, six months old when I go back to college? Day care won't be a problem. There's a great program at our church. My mom will love being able to see her first grandbaby whenever she wants."

Whoa—this was a little too much to be dealing with right now. "Speaking of my mom," she said, deciding for her own peace of mind she needed to shift topics. "She called today. She still wants to do a big party, but that's going to take some putting together. In the meantime, she would like to throw us a wedding shower. Probably just for girlfriends, if you don't mind."

His trapped expression cleared. "I think it's a good idea. You and your friends will have fun."

Typical guy, she thought with a smile. "But the thing is, we need to register. People are going to want to buy us gifts. I went through the kitchen and you already have everything. But there's only one set of china, so maybe something for special occasions?"

"I don't care about that kind of thing," he said. "Noelle, pick out what you'd like to have. Then you can take it with you when this is over."

The "this" being their marriage. "You're not interested at all?" she asked, a little surprised by how disappointed she felt.

"You'll have fun choosing things like china and sheets."

Not by herself, she thought glumly. Maybe Rachel or Crissy would want to help. But that wasn't the same as having Dev doing with it her. After all, he would be eating off the plates, too.

"I did have something I wanted to ask you," he said, setting down his fork and looking at her. "I should have brought this up before. Do you want to speak to a grief counselor about Jimmy?"

He wouldn't pick out china but he was offering her therapy? "I'm okay," she told him.

"I can get you some names. I wasn't sure, what with you having the baby and all."

"Thank you." She sipped her water. "I know Jimmy and I dated for a while and we, well, you know. He had talked about getting married and all, but…" She cleared her throat. "I don't think we were really in love with each other."

Dev stiffened in his chair. "We don't have to talk about that," he said gruffly.

He seemed uncomfortable. But why? Because she was being realistic about her relationship with his brother? Did that upset him? Did he want to believe they'd been madly in love? Or was he judging her for sleeping with a man without being sure she loved him?

"Dinner was great," he said as he rose and carried his plate to the counter. "I brought some work home, so I'll excuse myself."

And with that, he was gone. She didn't think she was going to see him again that evening.

Separate lives, she thought. That's what they were living. While she hadn't considered what their married lives would be like, she'd never thought she would be so…lonely. She felt lost in this big, beautiful house, living with a man who didn't want to have much to do with her. Lost and alone and not sure what to do about it.

Chapter Six

Dev arrived home nearly two hours early to find loud music filling the house. He walked into the family room and saw Noelle sprawled across the sofa, a large text book propped up as she slowly flipped through the pages.

Instead of the conservatively dressed woman he'd seen last night, today his wife of less than a week wore a tank top and shorts. Her feet were bare, her hair piled up on top of her head in a ponytail and she was chewing gum. She was, he acknowledged wryly, a teenage boy's dream.

Which meant he had no excuse for what *he* was feeling—he was old enough to know better.

Still, the information didn't seem to have any impact on the sudden rush of blood south or the desire to cross the room, pull her into his arms and kiss her senseless. He imagined her yielding and aroused, straining to get closer, reaching for him as they—

He forced the erotic images out of his mind. This was a marriage of practicality, he reminded himself. Nothing more. Besides, he'd been enough of an ass last night. He should take a break from that kind of behavior.

Pushing her to talk about Jimmy had been out of line and now that she'd admitted she didn't think she and his brother had been in love, he, Dev, felt even more like a jerk. He'd only done it to find out if she was in mourning or not. Knowing she wasn't overwhelmed by the loss of his brother meant, in a twisted way, that she was more available to him. Maybe *he* was the one who needed professional help.

He crossed to the CD player and turned down the volume. Noelle jumped. She sprang to her feet and the textbook hit the floor.

"Dev!" she said, obviously startled. "You're home early." She touched her hair, then fingered the hem of her tank top. "I'm not ready."

"You live here," he reminded her. "There's nothing to get ready for."

"Dinner," she said as she folded her arms over her chest. "I was going to get changed."

"You don't have to for me. I think you look charming."

She tried to smile, then failed. She reached up and pulled a band from her hair so that it tumbled loose around her shoulders.

The instant disarray was too sexy by far. Despite the steady hum of the air conditioner, he had the sudden need to unfasten his collar button and pull off his tie.

Instead he walked over to the large wrapped package he'd left by the entrance to the family room and held it out to her. "I brought you something."

Her gaze locked on the box and a her mouth curved into a wide grin. "Really? For me."

She tucked her hands behind her back, as if to keep herself from lunging toward the present.

"I felt badly about missing your birthday," he admitted. He started to apologize for the previous night, then stopped, not wanting to get into all that right now.

"You didn't have to get me anything," she said politely, even as she practically quivered in anticipation.

"You're not very good at this," he said, then set the package down on the coffee table. "You're *saying* all the right things, but I can tell you want to jump on the box and rip it open."

She looked at him and smiled. "I love surprises. I was always the first one up on Christmas morning. Even now, my parents have to set a time limit so I won't be downstairs, shaking boxes at five in the morning."

"No one is making you wait but you."

"If you're sure," she said even as she dropped to her knees in front of the coffee table and tugged at the wrappings. In a matter of seconds, she had the box open and was staring down at the sleek, silver laptop computer he'd bought her.

Dev perched on the edge of the overstuffed chair. "It's lightweight, so you can take it to classes, and wireless. We have wireless high-speed in the house, so you can be online just about anywhere. Even out by the pool."

She opened the top and ran her fingers over the keyboard. "Right. Because everyone wants to do e-mail poolside." She turned to him. "Dev, this is really, really nice. I don't know what to say."

He shrugged. "I didn't think you had one already."

"I don't. It's terrific. Thank you."

"You're welcome. I thought later we could go online and register somewhere. You know, for gifts."

Her eyes widened slightly and her lips parted, even though she didn't speak.

"I know you were disappointed last night," he admitted, feeling uncomfortable. "You surprised me. I hadn't thought about things like showers and parties. I shouldn't have left it all up to you."

A warm, happy smile blossomed on her face. She left the laptop and shifted to him, crossing the few feet of area rug still on her knees. Then she put her hands on his thighs, leaned in and kissed him on the mouth.

"Thank you," she said again. "In case no one has told you recently, you're a pretty great guy."

The soft pressure of her mouth lingered long after she'd pulled away. Desire exploded and he instinctively pulled away to help keep himself under control.

"Oh," she breathed as she stood and took a step back. "Sorry. I was just saying thank you. I didn't mean anything by…" She waved her hand vaguely in his direction.

Guilt ground into him. He swore silently. "Don't apologize," he told her gently. "We're married. Kissing is allowed."

"But you said you didn't want that for us. It wasn't part of the deal."

Sex. She was talking about sex. Something he wasn't going to experience again for a very long two years.

"I said I wasn't marrying you to pressure you into sleeping with me," he reminded her. "I didn't want you to feel obligated. We're living in the same house. We're going to run into each other. We need to get comfortable with that, and with kissing. As far as the world's concerned, we're newlyweds. We have to act like it."

"So my thank-you kiss was practice?" she asked.

There was something in her tone that made him wonder if she were holding in laughter. "If you want."

She sighed. "There are very complicated rules

here. It would help me a lot if we could get them in writing."

He saw the humor in her gaze. "I'll see what I can do," he told her. "Maybe someone could stitch them in a pillow for us."

"That would give our company something to talk about."

He could only imagine.

Determined to make things right between them, he crossed to her, put his hands on her shoulders, then bent down and lightly brushed his mouth against her.

"You're welcome," he said. "Happy birthday a little late."

This close he could see all the various colors of blue that made up her irises. Her lashes were surprisingly long and dark and there was a tiny freckle by the corner of her mouth.

He could hear the slight intake of air and feel the tension in her body. The very male part of him quickly pointed out that those were symptoms of a woman receptive to a man. That maybe, what with her not being wildly in love with Jimmy, she was open to getting involved with someone else—namely him.

Right—because he needed another disaster in his life. Noelle was wrong on so many levels. Most importantly, she was carrying his brother's child. Whatever might have happened in the future, Jimmy had been involved with her when he died, and it was still Dev's fault that his brother was dead.

"Thank you for my wonderful present," she said as he lowered his hands to his side. "I made peanut butter cookies earlier. Would you like some?"

"Sure. They're my favorite."

She grinned. "Mine, too."

She led the way into the kitchen.

Dev followed her and did his best to ignore the sway of her curved hips. Noelle was nothing like he'd imagined. She was a contradiction of terms. Still young and excited by presents, but mature and capable. Smart, funny and, as her mother had pointed out, not as tough as she thought. He would have to remember that. The last thing he wanted to do was hurt her.

"This place is huge," Lily said on Saturday morning as Noelle led her through the house. "I'm so jealous."

"No, you're not," Noelle told her. "You'd hate this. You like changing guys at least twice a month. I don't think you're going to be willing to settle down for years."

"That's true, but the house is great."

"Dev picked a really terrific decorator," Noelle said, having met the woman for the first time the previous week when she'd come to supervise the work on the pool house. "Some of the antiques belonged to his grandmother."

When Lily had called and said she wanted to come by, Noelle had been torn between welcoming a familiar face and not being sure she could handle the stress. She'd dropped by the church office twice the previous week so she could see her parents and ward off any plans for a surprise visit.

Having someone from her family in the house meant making sure there were no personal items showing in her bedroom and putting a few things on the dresser in Dev's room.

Complications, she thought as she and Lily finished their tour and headed out to the backyard to have snacks by the pool.

"If I just didn't have to be married, I could get into this," Lily said. She sipped her soda and reached for a tortilla chip from the bowl.

"Good thing you're going to college. You're going to need a really great job to support this lifestyle."

Lily wrinkled her nose. "I know. I'm still trying to decide what to study. You've known since your accident. Are you still going to be a nurse?"

Noelle nodded. "I start summer school on Monday. Calculus."

"Yuck," Lily said. "But aren't you supposed to be on your honeymoon?"

Whoops. Noelle thought fast. "This wasn't a good time for Dev to be away from work," she said with a casualness she didn't feel. "The wedding was a little impulsive, so we couldn't plan for stuff like that. We'll go later."

"Too bad. It would be great to be away on a beach somewhere with a good-looking guy. I wouldn't say no to that." She looked at her sister. "Okay, so tell me everything."

Noelle blinked at her. "About…"

"You know." Lily lowered her voice, then whispered, "Sex. Mom told us all kinds of things, but that's just logistics. I want details. Is it scary? Wonderful? Is it like in books? Do you see stars or feel swept away?"

Noelle felt herself blush. "I am *not* having this conversation with you," she said sternly. "It's not appropriate."

"I'm eighteen, and your sister. Come on. How am I supposed to find out about this if you won't tell me? You wouldn't want me experimenting just so I could know for myself," Lily added slyly.

"You're manipulating me," Noelle said.

"Forget it. I'm not going to talk about that. It's too personal."

In truth it wasn't personal at all. She simply didn't have anything to say. Her lone night with Jimmy had been a blur, first of pain, then of uncomfortable intimacy. In the few hours they'd been together, he'd entered her a number of times, but before she could figure out what he was doing or what was expected, it had been over.

Plus, he'd been so *heavy* when he collapsed on her. She'd felt trapped and embarrassed and frankly, she didn't get why everyone made such a big deal about it.

Dev stood just inside the family room, the sliding door open, one foot on the patio. He'd been about to go out and greet his new sister-in-law, but given the current topic, he decided a timely retreat was far more intelligent.

"At least tell me if it hurt the first time," Lily said. "I can't get a straight answer on that."

"It did," Noelle admitted. "It's a little awkward. I didn't know where to put my arms and stuff."

Lily winced. "But Dev made it okay, right? He talked you through everything."

"Yes, Dev was very patient and…and he made me laugh so I stopped being embarrassed. He made it great."

If he hadn't known better, even he would have been convinced by her words. But he *did* know better. Noelle was saying all the right things to convince her sister.

He stepped back into the house and quietly closed the slider. If Jimmy had been the typical twenty-year-old, Noelle's first and only night of passion probably hadn't been anything she remembered fondly. He, Dev, hadn't been anything great in bed at that age. He found himself wanting to apologize for something that wasn't his fault.

Later, when Lily left, he found Noelle in the kitchen.

"Did you enjoy having your sister drop by?" he asked.

She looked up from the vegetables she was chopping and smiled. "She's always fun."

"I started to come out on the patio to join you, but I heard what you were talking about," he said.

She frowned for a second, then blushed. "Oh. That."

"Thanks for the compliment."

Her mouth twisted in a half smile. "I had to say something. I couldn't admit my first time had been with Jimmy."

"Or that it hadn't been very good."

She set down the knife and looked at him. "How did you know?" she asked, sounding shocked. "Did he say anything? Did he tell you I was awful?"

"He didn't say a word. He didn't have to." Dev leaned against the counter. "It comes with the territory. Most young guys aren't great in bed. They haven't had the time to develop any skills, nor are they especially interested in anything but getting laid." He grinned sheepishly. "At twenty, it's all about getting laid."

She eyed him. "Even for you?"

"I wasn't always this smooth."

That made her smile. "Thanks for telling me. I wasn't sure what to think.... I didn't hate it, but it was…"

"Fast?" he asked wryly.

"A little. It hurt. I didn't bleed or anything, but there was a lot of pressure and stretching." She ducked her head. "I couldn't figure out where everything went and I wasn't comfortable asking questions."

Dev had never made love with a virgin, but he would guess her complete lack of experience would complicate an already difficult situation.

"Next time it will be better," he told her, refusing to picture the moment with Noelle. "As men get older, they learn a few things."

"Like?"

He shifted, not sure he wanted to get into this with her. Talking about sex made it too easy to imagine making love with her. He did his best to shut down that part of his brain. Unfortunately his body refused to cooperate.

"It takes longer."

She made a face. "And that's a good thing?"

He laughed. "Okay, let me start at the beginning. Once the need for volume fades a little, most men start to get interested in pleasing their partners. There are things a man can do to make a woman excited and passionate about the experience. Once that happens, then yes, lasting longer is a good thing."

She didn't look convinced. She opened her mouth, then closed it.

The smart move would be to end the conversation now…before he got too interested. But he liked Noelle too much to shut her down.

"If you can't ask me, who are you going to ask?" He shrugged. "What do you want to know?"

She looked at him. "So women do really have orgasms?" she asked, as color climbed up her cheeks.

"Sure. There are different ways of making that happen."

He had a sudden and powerful image of Noelle naked, her knees bent, legs pulled back as he kissed her intimately, his tongue swirling around the very heart of her arousal. He wanted to cross the kitchen, strip off her clothes and touch every part of her. He wanted to taste her and feel her quiver beneath him as she experienced her very first climax.

"How do you know it's happening?" she asked.

This was the strangest conversation he'd ever had. "If you have to ask, it *didn't* happen."

Despite her obvious embarrassment, she smiled. "That's not very helpful." She sighed. "I'll have to take your word for all this. I don't want to say anything bad about Jimmy, but that one night wasn't very thrilling. Given the choice, I'd never do that again. But if it could be different…"

He felt blood swelling in his groin at the thought of showing her the possibilities.

"You've been with a lot of women," she said.

A dangerous statement, he thought as he remained carefully quiet.

"Did they all like the sex part?"

"Yes."

"You can be sure?"

"Good question and my male ego says yes. To the best of my knowledge, they all did."

"So you can tell when a woman, uh…" The blush had returned, more fiery than ever.

"There are…physical manifestations."

She looked startled. "You can feel that with your…" She cleared her throat. "You can feel that?"

"Sometimes."

He didn't want to get into the fact that they were easier to feel with his fingers than his erection. That comment would only lead to a discussion on what his fingers would be doing inside of her.

"Maybe you could get a book or something," he said, wishing he could think of a good way to change the subject. If they kept this topic up much longer, she was going to notice his arousal and God knows what questions would follow then.

Noelle was far more curious than he'd realized. With his luck, she would want to see and touch and then they'd been in real trouble.

"I don't think I could go into a bookstore and buy something like that," she said.

"That's why we have the Internet." He paused. "Okay, then. I'll let you get back to what you were doing." He hurried from the kitchen and wondered how long it had been since he'd felt such a need for a woman, and if a cold shower would be any help at all.

"So," Crissy said with a grin. "You're married. How's that going?"

Noelle laughed, which was a mistake because three stitches slipped off her needles and when she tried to put them back, she pulled out half a row.

"Good," she said. "I mean, we're adjusting. Dev is great. He's really considerate and sweet. He didn't know it was my birthday and when he found out, he bought me a laptop."

Rachel sighed. "I really like that in a man.

Someone who respects a good appliance. So romantic."

"I thought it was a great gift," Noelle said defensively. "I can really use it at college and the one he picked is small and lightweight and has wireless Internet. This isn't a regular marriage. I didn't expect a romantic gift."

Rachel raised her eyebrows as she looked at Crissy. "She seems to be very protective of the new Mr. Noelle."

"I noticed that," Crissy said. "Interesting."

Noelle knew they were only teasing. "You're just jealous."

"A little," Rachel said. "Although last year one of my students brought me a baby white mouse for my birthday. It was very touching."

Crissy laughed. "I would have run screaming from the room, but that's just *moi*." She looked back at Noelle. "You're really doing okay? No weirdness?"

"The entire situation is weird. Dev is really great, but we don't know each other. I'm not sure what he expects from me or even what I expect from him. So far we're being very polite."

"Good manners are always helpful," Crissy offered. "I'm in favor of them."

"Well, he knows plenty. We're both trying. He even suggested I talk to a grief counselor about Jimmy if I thought I should." She put down her project and leaned forward. "I told him I was fine. The thing is, I don't feel like I need one. I missed Jimmy a lot at first, and I felt horrible after he died, but I'm not spending much time missing him." Not really any time, she thought glumly. "Is that natural? Am I an awful person?"

Rachel looked at her. "For the sake of humor, I want to say 'yes,' but as your friend, I'll tell the truth. Of course not. You feel what you feel. You guys didn't date that long. It was intense because he left and then came back. Noelle, you never promised to love him forever."

"But I slept with him."

Crissy sighed. "Honey, women have been messing up their lives by sleeping with the wrong guy for centuries. You did it, I did it, I'm sure Rachel will admit she's done it."

Rachel nodded.

"No one can be smart all the time," Crissy continued. "Circumstances change. We change. You make the best decision you can at the time and let it go."

"Like marrying Dev," Rachel added. "He sounds like a great guy. He's the closest thing to a biological father the baby is going to have so it really makes sense for you two to be together."

What they said sounded logical, Noelle thought. "I do like him," she admitted. "This entire situation could have been a nightmare, but he's gone out of his way to make things easy. I thought..." She smiled. "I thought we'd have nothing in common. I dreaded evenings, wondering what we'd talk about, but it's easy. We like a lot of the same kinds of movies and he loves peanut butter cookies, which are my favorite."

He'd even been willing to talk about sex with

her, although she wasn't going to share that with her friends.

"Uh-oh," Rachel said, glancing at Crissy. "I didn't see this coming."

"It was always a possibility," Crissy told her. "Close proximity, a shared interest, being part of an exciting event. There's a reason birth rates soar after a blackout."

Noelle stared at her friends. "What *are* the two of you talking about?"

"You, honey," Crissy said. "You've got it bad."

"Got what?" Noelle asked, not sure she wanted to know.

"You're falling for Dev," Rachel said kindly. "You have all the signs."

"What? No! I'm not. I just appreciate how great he is."

"Him being great is how it starts," Crissy said.

Noelle refused to believe they were right. She liked Dev—under the circumstances, who wouldn't? But it didn't mean anything.

"You're totally wrong," she said. "But even if

you're not, what's the big deal? We're married. Shouldn't I at least like the guy?"

"Only if he likes you back," Crissy said. "The two of you made some pretty specific ground rules. If only one of you is willing to break them, then heartache could be right around the corner. I'd hate to see that happen."

"I won't get hurt," Noelle said. "I like the guy, but that's not the same as falling in love with him."

"Keep it that way," Rachel said. "Love is tricky. Now if you're talking about breaking the no-sex rule, that's more interesting."

Noelle hated that she could already feel herself blushing. She cleared her throat. "Speaking of that," she said, trying to sound casual, "I've been thinking about us, you know, maybe…"

Rachel leaned forward. "Doing the wild thing?"

Noelle groaned. "Don't say that. It's just, Jimmy and I, well, it was just the one night and it wasn't very, you know, good."

"Now I feel about ninety years old," Crissy said with a sigh. "I can barely remember my

first time. Which isn't important. Look, technically, you're married. Of course you're welcome
to have sex with your husband. Just be careful.
You already like him. If he dazzles you in bed,
you won't have a chance."

"I don't believe that," Noelle said. "It's just a
bodily function."

"It can be a lot more," Rachel told her. "It can
be an expression of love that touches every part
of you. Crissy's right. Take care of yourself."

Noelle wasn't sure she agreed with their
advice. "I'm already pregnant. What's the worst
that could happen?"

Chapter Seven

The doctor's waiting room was bright, with beautiful prints of mothers holding babies and happy toddlers with balloons or kittens. The seats were comfortable, the music, soft and inspiring. Still it took every ounce of willpower for Noelle to stay in the chair and not run screaming into the night. Or in this case, the early afternoon.

"You're fidgeting," Dev said as he flipped through a parenting magazine.

"I'm nervous. I can't believe I'm here. I don't feel pregnant. I guess the truth hasn't sunk in.

Plus, I'm terrified. I don't want there to be anything wrong with the baby. But I'm not sure I even really get there *is* a baby. Still, I want him or her to be healthy and I know millions and millions of women have done this before, so what's the big deal. It's like the circle of life in *The Lion King,* right?"

Dev stared at her. "You're quoting a cartoon?"

"One works with what one has."

"I don't know that I'd go with that, but okay." He took her hand and gently squeezed her fingers. "I know you're scared and this is all new. Just remember—you're not in this alone, and yes, millions of other couples have gone through it, including our parents."

"I know. When I finally tell my mom, she'll be full of great advice. She had four babies in six years. Talk about a pro. She…" Noelle glanced at him. "You never talk about your parents."

"There's not that much to say," he told her. "My mom died when I was sixteen. A previously undiagnosed heart condition. What she had isn't genetic—it was just one of those things." He hesitated. "My dad had never been the responsible parent. He lasted about six weeks after her death, then took off. I never knew why, but now, looking back, I think it was guilt."

"About what?"

"How he treated her. She loved him more than I'd ever seen anyone love another person. She lived for him. She was great to Jimmy and me, but he had her heart. Everything changed the second he came home. Her smile was bright, her laughter easier. But he stayed gone a lot and when he wasn't there, she moved around like a shadow or a ghost. They used to fight about that—about him staying away so much. He wasn't one to take responsibility. He spent a lot of time hanging out with his friends and other people."

Other people? "You think he had affairs?"

Dev shrugged. "Maybe. I saw him with someone once, but he said she was the wife of a friend and he was helping her shop for her husband. I was never sure I believed him. After my mother died, I told him I'd never forgive him for killing her."

Noelle frowned. "You said it was a problem with her heart."

"It was, but I think she was happy to go because she'd lived her whole life loving someone who wouldn't love her back. Then he left—abandoned his family."

Dev was the most logical, practical person she knew. For him to say his mother, in essence, died of a broken heart, shocked her.

Equally difficult for her was the fact that he'd lost both parents within a few weeks of each other. Whatever problems his father might have had, how could he have abandoned his two sons?

"My grandfather moved right into the house," Dev said. "He was pushing seventy, but that didn't stop him from doing all the things our dad had never done—like playing ball and coming to school games and stuff. He always had time for me."

"He loved you," she said, seeing the truth in Dev's eyes.

"He was a good man."

Just like Dev, she thought, knowing she didn't ever have to worry about him walking out on her child. He was going to be there for both of them, no matter what.

When Dev had been twelve, he'd fallen out of a tree and had broken his arm so badly that part of the bone had stuck through the skin. There'd been enough blood to float a ship and, despite the pain, he hadn't felt the least bit woozy. But when he and Noelle left the doctor's office nearly forty minutes later, he had a bad feeling he was seconds from passing out.

They were both laden down with brochures, a couple of books, prescriptions for vitamins, reading lists and notes.

"I have a due date," she said as she walked beside him down the hallway. "That's good."

"Yes, it is."

"And she said everything is fine, so that makes me happy. It won't be long until we can hear a heartbeat. That's exciting."

"Very."

He concentrated on his breathing, knowing that passing out now wouldn't help anyone.

"Of course there's a lot to think about. I'm going to have to change my diet a little. And get more exercise. I mean I exercise a lot, but it's casual—not organized. I hadn't thought of prenatal yoga. I don't think I'm that bendy, but I could try."

"Trying would be good."

There was only the main reception area of the women's center, then they would be in the parking lot. Despite the summer heat, he couldn't wait to get outside and away from all this.

"Dev?"

"Yes?"

"Are you as scared as I am?"

He glanced at Noelle and saw terror in her blue eyes. Her mouth trembled and she looked as ready to bolt as he felt.

He stopped and faced her. "Too much information?"

"Oh, yeah. And those diagrams. One of my friends talked about the birthing process as having too many fluids and I have to say, I agree with her."

Some of his tension eased as he smiled. "You only have to do it," he said. "I may have to watch."

"Oh, sure. Because watching is so much worse than passing something the size of a bowling ball through something else the size of a pea."

His smile turned into a grin. "I'm not ready for this, either. I knew you were pregnant, but until this appointment…" He wasn't sure how to explain.

"The baby wasn't real."

"Right."

She sighed. "For me, either. It was a concept. Kind of like knowing the holidays are coming, but avoiding malls and shopping. A baby. There's going to be a real baby. I'm not ready for this. At least you've done it before."

"I haven't had a baby. Jimmy was six when my

mother died and then my grandfather took over. I'm only responsible for the last ten years of life."

Which had been, Dev acknowledged, a total disaster. If only he'd handled things differently, Jimmy wouldn't be dead right now.

"So neither of us knows what we're doing," she said as she started walking toward the foyer. "I hope no one tells the baby."

As they walked toward the exit, he spotted a large open kiosk filled with different brochures.

"Maybe they have some information over there," he said, turning in that direction.

"Or classes," Noelle said. "We could take a class. That would be great. I helped my mom with Tiffany a lot, but I don't remember very much of it."

They each started grabbing brochures. Noelle spotted a clipboard.

"Here's a parenting seminar for kids of all ages. Oh, look. The baby one's starting in a couple of weeks. We could take that."

"Sign me up," Dev said, wanting to take all of

them right now. He could still hear Jimmy yelling at him that he wasn't his father, and then running out of the house.

Dev had tried, but his best had fallen way short of his brother's needs. Even after the fact, looking back, he couldn't figure out where he'd gone so wrong. He was determined not to repeat those mistakes with Noelle's baby, but if he didn't know what they were, how could he avoid them?

They left the center and headed toward the parking lot. Ten feet from Dev's car, Noelle came to a stop and looked at him.

"I can't do this," she said frantically. "I mean I really can't. I'm not ready to have a baby. I'm too young and inexperienced. I'm panicking. You need to talk me down."

"I'm older and I'm panicked, too, so get in line."

"What? But you're so together."

"Not about this," he told her.

They stared at each other. Between them, they probably had every brochure ever printed on the subject of child birth and child rearing.

They each had a couple of books, along with lists of resources.

She drew in a deep breath. "Okay, so we should probably calm down. The baby won't be here for seven more months. We're smart and capable. We can prepare."

Her words made sense. "Plus it won't expect much when it's born. Food, clean diapers, a place to sleep."

"Exactly. So we're fine."

They dropped their bags, brochures and lists into the trunk then got into the car. Before he started the engine, he glanced at her.

"How many classes did you sign us up for?" he asked.

"I think three. Maybe four. They'll call to confirm."

"There were three baby classes?"

She cleared her throat. "Well, no. One of them was for toddlers, but I thought…"

The panic faded and when it did, reason returned. One corner of his mouth twitched and he imagined what they must have looked like, frantically grabbing every brochure and stuffing them into bags.

"Good thing they don't charge for the literature," he said, fighting laughter.

Her eyes brightened with humor. "That would be some bill. I'd have to go back to work."

"Or we could sell some furniture."

They were both smiling now. She started to chuckle.

"Okay, I'll admit it—I totally lost it. But you did, too."

He held up both hands. "I agree. I am not ready to be a father."

"Same here. The idea of a child using the 'm' word gives me the willies."

He stared into her beautiful face and touched her cheek. "You'll be a great mom. You have all the qualities."

"Thanks. I feel the same way about you being a dad."

Before he could tell her he'd already failed at

that, she added, "If I had to totally freak out over this, I'm glad it was with you."

"Me, too."

There was something about her smile and the way she gazed at him. Something that drew him closer until, without planning the move, he pressed his mouth against hers.

The kiss started out simply enough. Just lips touching. He continued to stroke her cheek, but that was okay because he meant it to be a friendly, comforting gesture. Nothing about the action was supposed to be sexual.

Then she shifted closer and tilted her head slightly. The invitation was clear and irresistible. Fire exploded inside him, fueled by a need that he could barely contain.

Before he could tell himself he shouldn't, he touched his tongue to her lower lip. Even as she put her hands on his shoulders, she parted for him.

Despite his growing desire, he moved slowly, wanting to give her time to back away, or at least give him a good hard slap. He traced the inside of her lower lip, feeling her smooth skin and tasting her sweetness. When she didn't pull back, he gently touched the tip of her tongue with his.

Delicious, exquisite torture, Noelle thought as Dev leisurely deepened their kiss. If she'd been a little more sure of herself, she would have taken things into her own hands, so to speak, but this *was* their first real kiss and as he'd been the one to initiate it, she figured he could set the pace.

In a way, moving so slowly was good. It gave her time to explore his shoulders and back, to feel the lean muscles there, and the heat of his body. She could breathe in the scent of him and imagine what it would be like if they kept on kissing.

At last he swept into her mouth and claimed her. She sighed in appreciation as he explored her mouth, leaving behind excited tingling everywhere he touched. One of his hands dropped to her shoulder, the other settled on her waist where the weight was oddly unsettling.

She had the oddest urge to move closer and maybe nudge his hand higher. She was so shocked to realize that she wanted his hand on her bare breast that she pulled back.

They stared at each other. His dark eyes were bright with a light she hadn't seen before. Passion, she wondered. Did he desire her?

What was up with her body? She'd kissed before—lots of times. But she couldn't recalling feeling quite so...melty afterward. And the breast thing? Where had that come from? Jimmy had been the first. It hadn't been that big a deal. She'd never *imagined* feeling his fingers on her bare skin.

Just the thought made her break out in goose bumps. As she rubbed her bare arms she realized that the light was fading in Dev's eyes. It was replaced by something that looked like concern...or worse...second thoughts.

He was going to apologize, she thought desperately. No. She couldn't stand that. The kiss had been too good.

"I'm starved," she said with a bright smile. "It's nearly noon. Do you have time to grab lunch before you head back to work?"

He blinked at the change of topic. For a second she thought he was going to push forward and insist on discussing the kiss, but then he smiled.

"Sure. What are you in the mood for?"

A week later, Noelle sat in Dev's study and pretended to review her calculus homework. He'd brought home a few reports he'd needed to look at before morning, so she'd joined him on the pretext of finishing up her homework.

In truth, she'd already finished, but she'd wanted to hang out with him and couldn't think of another excuse. Something had changed between them, at least for her, and she was still trying to figure out what it was.

She could pinpoint the exact date everything had shifted—it had been the afternoon of her first doctor's appointment. Sometimes she thought it was because he'd kissed her in a way she'd never been kissed before. Not that the style was all that different—it was more her own reaction that was keeping her up nights. Other times she told herself that while the kiss was nice, it didn't mean all that much. The real bonding had occurred over their shared revelation that they were really having a baby together. That this situation was about more than logistics and details—that there would be another *life* involved.

They'd laughed together, panicked together and had found comfort in sharing the experience.

Whatever the cause, Dev was no longer just Jimmy's older brother, the man who was being kind to her in desperate circumstances. He was his own person. Someone she liked and respected. Someone who could make her toes curl with a smile.

She had several dilemmas, she thought as she glanced up at him from her corner of his leather sofa. Had anything changed for him? Did he see her as only a problem to be solved, or was she a real person? She thought he liked her well enough, but she wanted more than that. She wanted him to find her sexy and attractive and exciting.

She sighed. She could rate attractive easily enough on a good day, but sexy and exciting weren't words usually used around her.

There was also the age difference. She knew he was aware of it. So did he find her too young? She thought she was doing a good job of holding her own with him, but that was just from her perspective. So what did he think?

Her mother had always told her it was much better to ask than wonder, that being straightforward was the best way to make a relationship work. The advice seemed sound, but the thought of putting it into practice terrified her. Wishing and dreaming were totally safe. Acting was something else entirely.

What if he completely rejected her? What if he thought she was stupid? What if he laughed at her?

Dev looked up and caught her staring at him. He raised his dark eyebrows. "What?" he asked.

"Nothing."

"It's something. You were scowling."

She grinned. "I do not scowl. It's not ladylike and I was brought up to be a lady."

"Fine. You were pensive. Want to tell me why?"

She bit down on her lower lip and wondered if she had the courage to be honest. Or at least semihonest. "I was wondering about the other women in your life."

The eyebrows went a little higher and he leaned back in his chair. "I take it the calculus homework isn't challenging enough to keep your brain occupied."

"Not tonight."

"And the most interesting topic you could come up with was the women in my life?"

"Uh-huh."

"You need to get out more."

She laughed. "Come on, Dev. We're married. You can tell me."

"One might think telling one's wife was exactly the *wrong* thing to do. Besides, there aren't any other women. I told you I would be faithful."

A fact she was appreciating more and more. "I didn't mean now," she told him. "I meant before. There was only one serious relationship in my life and you know all about him. I think it's only fair to share information."

"Of course you do." He frowned. "I knew Jimmy was your first time, but do you also consider him your first serious relationship?"

She thought about the question. "I think so. There were guys I liked and dated. I actually went out a lot in high school. But I never really fell in love. I think a lot of it was the guys I dated knew my dad and were concerned about doing the wrong thing. I was always aware of being the preacher's daughter, as well. So I would kind of hold back and I think the guys did, too. So I guess that makes Jimmy my first serious relationship."

And she hadn't even been in love with him,

she thought sadly. What did that say about her decision-making skills?

"How did you and Jimmy meet?" Dev asked.

"He was visiting work for some reason. I was in the lunch room and he walked in. We just started talking." She thought about that first day. Jimmy had been good-looking, funny and, in some ways, more grown-up than the guys she was used to. "He didn't know anything about me, which I liked. He asked me out and I said yes."

Dev nodded slowly. "Jimmy always was a charmer with the ladies."

She wrinkled her nose. "You're saying I was one of many."

"As far as I know, you're the only one he talked about marrying."

She nodded, as if the statement had significance. She wanted to believe it was true but… "Dev, is it possible he just said that to get me to sleep with him?"

"Why do you ask?"

"I don't know. I've been wondering. Jimmy

was a great guy, but until he decided to go into the military, he seemed scattered. He had a million ideas about what he wanted to do, but none of them made sense. He wasn't a doer, really." She paused. "I'm sorry. I shouldn't talk about him this way with you."

"It's fine. I'm aware of Jimmy's faults." He picked up a pen, then put it back on his desk. "You're right. He was a dreamer."

She noticed he didn't answer her question— as to whether it was possible that Jimmy had just said he wanted to marry her to get her into bed. If he'd believed Jimmy really cared, he would have said so. Was he trying to protect his brother's reputation or her?

Knowing Dev as she did, she thought it might be both. Maybe she should just go with that and not try to second guess the past. There was no way of knowing now.

"You never told me about the other women in your life, although changing the subject to Jimmy was a neat trick."

"You like that? I could do it again." He shifted in his seat. "What do you want to know? There's nothing much to tell. I was a single guy who dated."

"There's more to it than that," she said. "They were all beautiful."

"You don't know that."

"I do. I saw a couple myself and Katherine told me."

He groaned. "Great. My own staff turns on me."

"We consider your personal life a hobby. You should be flattered."

"Amazingly, I'm not." He looked at her. "What else did she say?"

Noelle pretended to study her nails. "Nothing really. But we found it fascinating that you always chose exotic beauties. No milkmaids for you."

He laughed. "Milkmaids?"

"You know—traditional looking. Blond hair, blue eyes."

"Like you."

She shrugged. "I could fall into the milk-maid category."

"So you'd believe me if I told you that I thought you were beautiful, but you'd draw the line at exotic?"

He thought she was beautiful? Noelle wanted to stand up and cheer. Except he hadn't said that, exactly. There'd been an "if" in that sentence.

"I'm no one's definition of exotic," she said. "I can live with that. So about these women."

He closed his eyes. "I can't believe you're seriously interested in them. So why don't you ask what you really want to know?"

Hmmm, there was a concept. She drew in a breath, squared her shoulders and blurted out, "What do you know that Jimmy didn't? About sex, I mean."

Dev had braced himself, but even so, the question caught him like a shot. He felt emotionally flung back in his seat and left for dead.

Couldn't she have just asked to buy new bedroom furniture?

He swore silently. This was *not* a conversation they should be having. He had an entire list of reasons as to why not. The most pressing was that he'd spent the last week doing his damnedest to avoid any remotely personal contact with Noelle. He'd been interested before, but kissing her had shown him there were plenty of possibilities and now they were driving him crazy.

He wanted her. He'd wanted other women before and kept trying to tell himself this was an itch that would fade with time. But whenever he got the need under control, he found himself catching sight of the curve of her cheek or the back of her thighs as she pranced around the house in shorts.

Worse, sometimes she got him by just talking. She would spout an opinion on some world event that surprised him, not only with her view, but with the facts she had to back it up. He'd caught her reading a science magazine two days after she'd admitting to having a weakness for celebrity gossip tabloids. How was he not supposed to adore that?

"You're stalling," she said.

"I'm considering my options."

"Why is the question so difficult? It's just information."

He shook his head. "It's more than that and you know it." What to say? "What I know that Jimmy didn't isn't important. Just a few details."

"Life is in the details," she told him. "What are you afraid of?"

Going where he shouldn't, he thought grimly. Wanting too much.

She glanced at the carpet, then back at him. "Dev, we're married and we plan on staying married for the next two years. That's kind of a long time. I know you had a…physical relationship with the other women in your life. It's a natural part of life. While I appreciate your promise to be faithful for the time we're married, I think you're setting yourself up for a lot of un-necessary suffering."

She raised her head and gazed directly at him. "I like to think we're becoming friends, which is an odd thing to say, considering the fact that we're married, but this is an odd situation. I don't want you to break your promise to be faithful and I don't want you to do without. I'm willing to be your wife in that way, too."

He heard the words, but he couldn't believe them. She was supposed to be the innocent in all this—how the hell had she figured it all out?

"A generous offer, but not one you need to make," he said gruffly.

"Really?" She smiled. "So you're just going to ignore that part of your life? It's not like the need goes away. My parents have been married more than twenty years and they're still hot for each other." Her smile turned into a grin. "When I was a teenager, I was so uncomfortable, knowing they did that. I mean, they're parents. But now I see their intimacy as a really good thing. It helps keep the relationship strong."

He had no idea what to say to her.

Noelle pulled her knees to her chest. "I'll admit my lone experience wasn't anything I'd want to repeat, but you said it could be better and I trust you. So if you're interested, I'm willing."

There were two spots of color on her face, but otherwise she seemed completely calm and in control. Amazing, he thought, still stunned at her courage and honesty.

"Unless you don't want me," she added, as she ducked her head.

Not want her? "Noelle, don't go there," he told her. "Wanting has nothing to do with it."

"Then it's because I'm pregnant. Does that gross you out?"

That made him smile. Nothing about her "grossed him out." She only had to be breathing for him to want her. "You being pregnant isn't an issue." He felt uncomfortable and wasn't sure why. A beautiful woman was offering herself to him. Shouldn't that be a *good* thing?

It was, except he wasn't sure it was right for her. She'd only been with one of guy and he'd been Dev's brother. The situation was twisted in ways he couldn't describe.

There was also his concern about what would happen after. If they did become lovers. The women he let into his life understood the rules—no permanent entanglements. Despite the two-year contract they had, he wasn't sure Noelle could be his lover and walk away.

She stood. "I can see you're not ready. That's fine. I'll wait. But the offer remains open."

Then she walked out.

He was left with an aching need and no clue as to what to say. What the hell was wrong with this picture? What was he supposed to do now? Go after her? Pretend they'd never had this conversation? He'd been left hanging in the wind by a twenty-year-old innocent.

If this had happened to anyone else, he would think it was the funniest thing he'd ever seen.

Chapter Eight

Dev found himself in the unusual position of being nervous about walking into his own house. Every since he and Noelle had had what he thought of as the "sex talk," he'd half expected to find her waiting for him wearing a big, red bow and nothing else.

While nearly every part of his brain and body would kill for such a thing to happen, the lone sensible cells still functioning pointed out that there were massive problems to be had should he and Noelle become lovers.

She was pregnant by his brother. She had neither the temperament nor the experience of his usual temporary women and might not fully understand the rules. This was supposed to be a sensible arrangement in the best interests of Noelle and the baby. He was confident there was no way to justify an intimate relationship as beneficial to either.

That said, he couldn't help wanting her. Worse, the longer he knew her and learned more about who she was, the *more* he wanted her. He'd had relationships that started out with great promise only to fade into nothing very quickly. With Noelle, it was the opposite. He hadn't had any expectations about her when they'd first made their arrangement, but the more he was around her, the more he admired and respected her.

Nearly a week after their uncomfortable conversation, he walked into the kitchen, once again braced for overt seduction or more questions, only to find her dancing in front of the stove, while a country song played on the radio.

Last night she'd been swaying to classical, the

night before she'd been bebopping to music from the 1940s. Noelle had many qualities, but she was never boring.

"Hi," she called when she saw him, then reached for the remote to the Bose system and turned down the volume. "Dinner will be ready in about ten minutes, if you want to go change."

She smiled as she spoke, then crossed to where he stood, placed one hand on his shoulder and brushed her mouth against his.

The kiss was light, nearly impersonal and left him panting for more. Then she turned back to the stove.

"I'm making chicken Marsala. I found a bottle of Marsala in the pantry, which is good because I couldn't buy it. This is my mom's recipe and it's fabulous, so I hope you're hungry."

He stood riveted to the floor. If he didn't know better, he would swear he was being seduced by his own wife, who wasn't even old enough to buy cooking wine.

"Starving," he muttered, not quite meaning

the food. "I'll go get changed and be back in five minutes."

"Good." She beamed at him, then cranked up the volume on the radio and resumed her dancing in front of the stove.

An hour later, they'd finished dinner and cleaned up the kitchen together. That was their new pattern. He wasn't sure when he'd decided to pitch in, but now every night he cleared the table and loaded the dishwasher while she wiped off the counters and the stove.

"Do you have homework?" he asked when they were finished.

She shook her head. "I'm all done for the day. I'm sure there will be more tomorrow. What about you? Anything from the office?"

"No," he said, then wished he hadn't. Time suddenly seemed to hang heavily on their hands.

"Then I have something I'd like to discuss."

As she spoke, she led the way to the family room. Dev thought briefly about ducking into his office, but he refused to be intimidated by the thought of a personal conversation. As long as the topic wasn't sex, he would be fine.

Noelle plopped onto the sofa, her long bare legs stretching out in front of her as she rested her heels on the coffee table. She wore shorts and a tank top, which left far too much skin bare. Her hair was loose, her toes painted pink and her smile just welcoming enough to make his blood heat.

"I've been thinking about what we talked about before," she said when he'd settled at the far end of the sofa.

He held in a groan.

"Is it Jimmy?" she asked. "Because I was with him?"

He had the realization that she was never going to let the topic go. Apparently the only way to stop talking about why they weren't having sex was to just go ahead and have it. Under any other circumstances, he would have given in.

"Jimmy is a factor," he admitted. "I still think of you as Jimmy's girl."

She nodded slowly. "I think if he hadn't died, you would have been more comfortable letting that relationship go. As it is, I'm the last person you know who was close to him. If you change that by getting close to me yourself, you lose that connection."

Her insights surprised him. "I hadn't put the concept into words, but you're right."

"So if you were to get involved with me, you'd be hurting your brother," she said.

He hesitated. He could sense danger down this conversational path, even though he couldn't see it. "I wouldn't say hurting," he told her. "The situation raises some questions."

"You know I'm not in love with him," she said.

He swore silently. "Yes, I know. Neither of us know what would have happened if Jimmy hadn't died."

He knew he would have forced his kid brother to do the right thing and marry Noelle, but he had his doubts about how long the relationship would have lasted.

She sighed. "This must be so hard for you," she said. "I only knew Jimmy a few months, but he's been a part of your world for twenty years. You're dealing with his loss and my pregnancy and me. I don't mean to pressure you, Dev. I don't want to make you uncomfortable. Considering the circumstances, I think we're doing really well."

"I do, too," he said. "And you're not making me uncomfortable."

She smiled. "Good to know." Her smile faded. "On the intimacy thing, I like you. I'll admit to some curiosity. Your reputation precedes you, which is intriguing. Honestly, your idea of being faithful and celibate for the next two years is really noble, but not very practical. I hate the thought of you suffering because you feel it's the right thing to do. I wouldn't normally be pushing on something like this, but there is a time factor. I'll be showing soon and I'm not sure we need my growing pregnancy as a complication."

Honest to God, he didn't know what to say. Even as a blush stole up Noelle's cheeks, she kept her gaze fixed firmly on his face. She might be embarrassed, but she wasn't backing down. How was that possible?

As for responding to her statement/offer—how? Of course he hated the idea of doing without for so long. Of course he was tempted by her words, her body and everything else about her. He had a feeling he could be beaten and left for dead on the side of the road and he would still want her.

But there were things too consider. Her innocence and the circumstances. Unfortunately, blood was heading south, leaving his brain in a deficient state, his cognitive abilities fading fast.

"I just…" He cleared his throat. "There are complications already," he muttered as he rose. "You're going to have to trust me on that. I, ah, I have some work I need to deal with."

And with that pitiful excuse, he left the room.

Noelle waited two more days before making her move. She told herself it was to give Dev time to figure everything out on his own, but in truth, she needed to think things through and gather her courage.

The entire situation was outside of her comfort zone, not to mention her experience level. Maybe she should just let it go. But a little voice in her head said that if she wanted to make her relationship with Dev stronger, this was what they needed. Making love would bond them and they would need that connection when the baby came.

There was also a part of her that was wildly curious about those differences he'd talked about and the things he knew that Jimmy hadn't. How would the experience be with him? How would he touch her and hold her and kiss her?

They'd already had that one great experience in the car. She'd found herself melting in his embrace and that was just a kiss. What would happen if things got serious?

She asked the question as she stood in front of her dresser and considered her seduction options. Because that's what she'd decided to do—seduce her husband.

She'd scanned a couple of books on the subject in the bookstore, secretively pulling the volumes from their proper place, then darting over to the classic literature corner where she could read in peace. Of course she hadn't totally been able to concentrate, what with her guilt and embarrassment on the subject.

To make up for that, she'd spent twice as much money on several cookbooks and then had ducked back to her car, hoping no one had seen her.

Now she was armed with a little information and a lot of questions, along with a vague idea of how to seduce a man. Unfortunately she didn't have any practical experience to add to the mix.

One of the books suggested showing up naked in bed. Noelle knew that the earth's rotation would have to change direction before she had the courage to try that. But the showing up in bed part of the idea had some merit. Somehow slipping between Dev's sheets and waiting silently seemed a whole lot easier than talking about what she was trying to do. Her mother had always told her, when in doubt, try the direct approach. Not that her mother had ever imagined a situation like this, Noelle was sure.

Okay, so she would boldly climb into his bed…while he was in the bathroom, of course. She didn't want him to know she was there until it was too late.

That problem solved, she turned to the next pressing issue—what to wear. She didn't have any sexy lingerie. While she had a couple of cute sets of summer pj's, she wasn't sure they set the right tone. Which left her with one short, pale pink nightgown. It was sleeveless and covered in tiny white flowers and came to the middle of her thigh.

She undressed, then pulled on the nightie. Next she brushed her hair, then her teeth, then changed into a pair of high-cut bikini panties instead of her regular bikini panties. After that, she ran out of things to do, so she left her bedroom and walked down the hall to the master suite.

She could hear the shower running in the bathroom so she stepped into the quiet, darkened room and headed directly for the bed.

Dev had already pulled off the heavy bedspread. The TV in the armoire was tuned to a twenty-four-hour news channel. She found the remote and turned off the TV, then faced the bed.

It was huge and high and her stomach flipped over as she stood there staring at the vast expanse of mattress. Could she really do this?

Her courage nearly failed her, but she forced herself to move steadily forward until she could put her hands on the smooth sheets. It was now or never, she thought, wishing she had more experience or was more convinced that Dev really wanted to make love with her.

Maybe he'd turned down all her offers because he didn't find her sexy enough. Maybe the pregnancy thing, or the fact that she'd slept with his brother, freaked him out more than he wanted to admit. Maybe that incredible kiss in the car had been about guilt or pity or…

She'd been so caught up in her worrying, that she hadn't heard the water turn off or heard Dev get out of the shower and dry off. But he must have because she heard him say her name and when she turned he was standing in the doorway to the bathroom and wearing nothing but a pair of silky-looking boxer shorts.

His dark eyes gave nothing away and she had no idea what he was thinking. She felt exposed and stupid and near tears as she confessed all.

"I read a book at the bookstore on how to seduce a man. It said to just get into your bed, naked. I couldn't do the naked part. It's really not me, and we don't know each other that well. So I had to find a nightgown, but I don't have sexy lingerie and until I got here I hadn't thought about the fact that you're probably not doing anything with me because you don't think of me that way. I'm not like those other women, and I'm pregnant and…"

She'd run out of words, which could be a first, but she didn't think that mattered right now. Fear and embarrassment and a sense of vulnerability welled up inside of her until she could only turn and run for the door.

Except she didn't get that far. Somehow Dev got from the bathroom doorway to her side before she could move and then she was in his arms and he was kissing her all over her face.

"It wasn't that I didn't want you," he breathed as he pressed his mouth to her cheeks, her eyelids, her nose and her chin.

"Then what was it?"

"Hell if I know."

He claimed her lips with a deep, passionate kiss that chased all rational thought from her mind. The fears faded, the questions were no more. She gave herself up to the pressure and the minty taste of his tongue as it circled hers and plunged in deeper.

As she angled her head to let him claim her, she placed her hands on his shoulders. His skin was warm and smooth. Muscles rippled as she slid her fingers down his back, then up again.

He cupped her face, as if he felt the need to hold her in place. Had she been willing to break the kiss, she would have told him that she wasn't going anywhere. Instead she tried to show him with her body by leaning against him and by her kiss. She thrust into his mouth and explored him until she felt herself wanting more.

Need grew inside. At least she was pretty sure it was need. Her breasts ached and the feel of the cotton gown on her bare breasts was both erotic and uncomfortable. There was a heaviness between her legs. Her thighs trembled and her skin seemed too tight for her body.

Without warning, Dev stepped away. Before she could protest, he caught her in his arms and carried her the few feet to the bed. There he lowered her onto the cool sheets, then settled next to her, leaning over her as he once again rained kisses on her face.

She touched him. His shoulders, his arms, then the breadth of his chest. His skin was smooth to her touch, but not soft like her own.

He was all hard planes and unyielding strength. He felt different than Jimmy had. Jimmy had been skinny and…well…different.

She closed her mind to anyone but Dev, then arched her head back on the pillow when he kissed his way along her jaw and down her neck. She wouldn't have thought that part of her body was especially sensitive, but when his damp kisses trailed to her collarbone, she felt goose bumps on her arms.

He knelt on the bed, then crossed over her, pulling her with him as he went so somehow she landed on top of him, their bodies pressed together. She looked down at him and saw the bright fire in his eyes. Her muscles clenched instinctively and when she moved, she felt the hardness of his arousal against her body.

The physical proof of his need gave her courage and excited her. She leaned in for his kiss as he claimed her in another dance of lips and tongues. He moved his hands down her back to her hips, where he silently urged her to straddle him. She parted her legs and shifted so that her center pressed against his erection.

The contact was shocking, yet delicious. Her insides ached, but not from pain. She wasn't sure of the cause or how to fix it. Instinctively, she rubbed herself against him, then stopped as tiny bolts of lightning shot through her body.

"Do that again," Dev breathed.

She raised herself and moved her hips back and forth, moving her center the entire, thick length of him. Pleasure poured through her and the need to do more nearly overwhelmed her. But before she could get started, he brought his hands to her breasts and cupped her curves.

They were covered by nothing more than a thin layer of soft cotton. She could feel his fingers, his thumbs, his palms. His gentle touch made her breath catch. Then he brushed his fingers against her nipples and she gasped.

It was as if a road of nerves connected her breasts with that place between her legs. As he continued to touch her nipples, circling them, lightly rubbing them, moving back and forth, she felt a distinct tugging deep inside. Muscles tensed and the need to rub herself against him harder and faster nearly overwhelmed her.

Dev reached for the hem of her nightgown and before she could figure out what he was doing, he swept it over her head. She instinctively reached to cover herself, but he got there first. He shifted her onto her back on the bed, bent over her and took her right nipple in his mouth.

A moan of pure pleasure started low in her belly and worked its way up. The combination of heat and dampness and the magical way he flicked and swirled and sucked nearly drove her to madness. It took every ounce of control to keep from grabbing his head and holding him in place. He must never stop. If he did—she would die.

Fortunately he continued to caress her breast with his mouth and tongue. At the same time, he put his hand on her stomach and slowly moved it toward her panties. When he encountered the barrier, he slipped under the fabric, moving until he slipped between her legs.

Jimmy had touched her there, she thought, remembering the few seconds of rough rubbing before he'd entered her. Dev was different. He went slowly, easing down between swollen flesh, making her anticipate his next move.

Without thinking, she parted her legs. He continued exploring her, touching everywhere, pressing lightly. It was nice, she thought. Very different from—

A bolt of pleasure jerked the breath from her body. She had never felt anything like it before and wasn't sure what—

It happened again. Dev slipped his fingers inside of her, then brought them back to that one tiny place. He circled it over and over again, moving closer but not touching until she felt she wanted to scream. He had to do that again. She had to know what it felt like if he kept stroking her.

But instead of continuing, he raised himself on

his elbow and smiled at her. "Take off your panties."

Five minutes ago, she might have been embarrassed. Now she didn't care. If a lack of panties meant he'd do that again, she was all for it.

She pushed off the scrap of fabric, then kicked it away. He stretched out next to her and began to kiss her mouth. As their tongues danced, she felt his fingers return between her legs.

He went right for that one spot and rubbed it. His fingers moved in an ever-increasing rhythm until she found herself lost in a haze of desire and need. Everything he did felt so good and she never wanted it to stop, yet she felt herself straining for something more. Something that was just out of reach.

She began to pulse her hips, as if urging him on. She opened her legs wider, then held onto the sheets. He moved faster and faster until her entire body throbbed with need.

When she didn't think she could stand it much longer, there was a single moment of stillness, then an unbelievable wave of pleasure swept through her. It was as if every part of her trembled with delight. She couldn't control herself or her reaction. She wanted to scream. She wanted to be more naked, more exposed, more everything. Her muscles contracted over and over again.

And still Dev touched her. He moved slower and lighter until the trembling eased and amazing contentment flowed into her.

He stopped moving, but kept his hand between her legs. She opened her eyes and found him staring down at her.

"Wow," she managed, her voice husky and low. "Was that what I think it was?"

He smiled. "Uh-huh."

"You could feel it, too?"

"I could tell by your breathing and the way your muscles contracted. If I'd been inside of you, I would have felt even more."

Inside of her? "How would that have felt for me?"

"I don't have a clue."

She grinned. "Right. Because you're the guy." Her smile faded. "I had no idea it could be like that. If it feels half as good for you when you, well, you know, why on earth would you have resisted for so long?"

"I was trying to do the right thing."

She touched his cheek. "Silly man."

"I've been called worse."

He bent down and kissed her. She'd thought he might protest taking things further and was pleased when he moved close and she felt his arousal against her thigh.

As she kissed him and rubbed her hands up and down his back, he tugged off his boxers, then knelt between her thighs. She felt him pressing against her. Instinctively she braced herself for the painful stretching, but it never came. She felt a slight pressure as he filled her, which actually felt kind of nice.

He filled her completely, moving slowly in and out of her. His weight felt comfortable, safe and a little sexy. She was aware of being female and the power contained in that. This was her husband, she thought as a little tingle shot through her. They were making love.

He began to move faster. Her body clenched around him and she felt the beginning of the same pressure she remembered from before. Was it possible she could climax again? Like this?

But before she could decide, he stiffened and groaned. She felt him go still.

Five minutes later, they were under the covers. Neither of them had pulled on clothes, which meant they were naked. She'd never slept naked before. Not that she felt sleepy.

"I have some questions," she said as she snuggled close, feeling at one with the universe.

"Ask anything."

"Are you sure? Some of them are personal."

He looked at her and smiled. "More personal than what we just did?" he asked, his voice teasing.

"They're on the same subject."

"I guessed as much. What do you want to know?"

"How come it didn't hurt?" she asked. "Last time it was so painful. This time I felt pressure and stretching, but it wasn't close to the same."

Dev stroked her hair. "You weren't a virgin, which helped. Plus, you were aroused. When you get turned on, your body changes. You get swollen and wet."

She'd thought things felt different "down there" but hadn't had much frame of reference. Knowing the mechanics and having them happen were not the same.

"It didn't last much longer," she said. "But I felt some tingling when you were inside. Could I, um, you know, that way?"

Dev groaned. "Next time it'll last longer. It's been a while for me, okay? Plus, I've been fantasizing about this for weeks."

She turned toward him, which meant her bare breasts brushed against his arm. The contact was so unexpected, she nearly lost her train of thought. "What are you talking about?"

"I didn't last long enough. Guys don't like to hear that."

How stupid. As if he could control those feelings. "Whatever. Could I?"

"Maybe. With practice."

Practice? That sounded yummy.

His words replayed in her mind. "You've been fantasizing about me? Really? Like what?"

"Like everything." His dark gaze brightened with fire. "I've been thinking about touching you, tasting you. Being together everywhere. The kitchen counter, this bed, the pool."

The pool? People did that? She felt both shocked and excited by his words. Who would ever have thought that calm, responsible, mature Devlin Hunter was so sexy?

"I'm not sure I could get naked in the pool during the day," she said, ignoring the blush on her cheeks. "But I'm willing to try it at night."

He claimed her with a kiss that made her

wish he would touch her again. Instead he pulled back.

"You're one surprise after the other," he told her.

"But in a good way."

He rubbed his thumb across her mouth. "In the best way. We'll do it all, I promise. But not tonight. I don't want you sore tomorrow."

He drew her close again. She put her head on his shoulder and rested her hand on his chest. Sleep was impossible, but she liked being close to him. She liked knowing what they'd done and that he'd wanted her for a long time.

"I wanted you, too," she whispered.

"I'm glad."

Crissy nudged Rachel. "Is it just me or is that one glowing?"

Rachel narrowed her gaze as she looked at Noelle. "She is. Worse, she can't seem to stop smiling. Think she won the lotto?"

Noelle tried for a serious expression, but she was just too happy. This morning, at her calculus class, several people had commented on her extraordinary mood. She hadn't told them the cause, but she was happy to share the news with her friends.

"It's Dev," she said, then sighed. "We're together."

Rachel nodded knowingly. "That's code-speak for getting some."

"I haven't had some in a while," Crissy said. "I could use some."

Noelle grinned. "I would highly recommend it."

"Better than the first time?" Rachel asked.

"Totally different. Dev was fabulous. Patient and sexy and the things he can do."

Crissy fanned herself with her hand. "Is it me, or is it getting hot in here?"

"It's not you," Rachel said, sounding grumpy.

Noelle ignored their teasing. "I'm so happy. I can't believe this has happened to me. I married Dev because it seemed the only way to deal with the baby and now…it's just amazing. I feel so connected to him. Is that natural."

Rachel nodded. "Women bond after sex."

"I feel it," Noelle said dreamily. "I can't stop thinking about him or wanting to be with him. I thought our marriage would be nothing but a duty. Now it's so much more."

Rachel and Crissy looked at each other. "Be careful, honey," Crissy told her. "You're new to all this. Dev, making love… Don't go getting your heart all soft and open until you know what his intentions are."

Noelle laughed. "He married me."

"For two years," Rachel reminded her.

Noelle dismissed them with a wave. "You don't understand. We shared something special. The more I've gotten to know him, the more I've liked him. Now…" She sighed again. "I don't know how I got so lucky. And you know the best part? We're already married."

Dev walked into the kitchen, still not sure what he was going to say to Noelle. While last night had been great, it had also been a mistake.

He didn't want to hurt her, and in his gut, he knew that being lovers was the shortest path to that happening.

He'd spent the entire day and all of his dinner meeting wrestling with guilt. How could he have done that? How could he have given in? He wasn't supposed to be enjoying himself. Noelle was nothing but a responsibility. He was helping her because of Jimmy and the baby.

Noelle greeted him with a kiss that heated his blood. In that moment, with her body pressed against his, it was all he could do not to push her onto the counter and have his way with her again.

Instead, he forced himself to step back as he tried to figure out how to tell her they weren't going to do that again.

"Come see, come see," she said as she took his hand and dragged him toward the hallway. "I know I should have asked, and I would have, but you were having that dinner meeting. I got home from my knitting class about an hour ago and I just couldn't help myself. Are you mad?"

Her eyes were bright, her smile infectious. How could he possibly refuse her anything. "As I have no idea what you're talking about, I guess the answer is no."

"What? Oh, right." She laughed. "This way."

She drew him into the bedroom. "I rearranged the drawers. I only took four in the main dresser, plus the nightstand on the other side. The closet was easy. You're not even using half of it."

She pulled open the wide door to show him her clothes hanging next to his. She'd moved into his bedroom.

"I know we didn't talk about this," she said. "But after last night, it made the most sense. I'll keep the same room for the nursery. With a baby monitor, I'll be able to hear everything."

She stepped into his arms. He put his hands on her shoulders and stared into her eyes.

"Say something," she whispered. "Please."

He didn't want this. Oh, sure, he wanted *her,* and what man would object to a beautiful, sexy woman in his bed on a regular basis?

But everything had a price and he didn't want her paying this one. He didn't want them to get closer. He didn't want her to care. He wasn't worried about himself—he'd already learned he was immune to love, but Noelle wasn't.

"We should…" he began as she reached for the hem of her T-shirt and pulled it over her head.

"What?" she asked. She took his hands and placed them on her breasts. "Make love this instant?"

She was the most amazing woman he'd ever met. Funny, smart, impulsive, responsible, sexy, adoring. In other circumstances…

But these weren't other circumstances, and if she knew the truth about him, she would never forgive him.

Walking away would be the kindest thing. He knew that and yet he found himself unable to resist her invitation. When she smiled and raised herself on tiptoe, he bent his head and claimed her.

Tomorrow, he promised. He would tell her the truth tomorrow.

Chapter Nine

"What terrifies everyone about babies is they can't tell you what's wrong," the attractive middle-aged woman said from the front of the room. "At least not verbally. The good news is, babies have simple needs. They want to be fed, kept comfortable and clean and not feel pain. So it's not as if you have to worry that your newborn is feeling unfulfilled by his or her job."

The woman paused expectantly, and a few people laughed. Dev didn't join in. To him, the joke wasn't funny. He was here to learn how to be a decent parent—something he'd never accomplished with Jimmy.

Dev knew the woman was right—at the beginning the baby's needs would be basic and mostly physical. He was unlikely to do any psychological harm. But what about as it got older? Then what?

"For the first couple of months, you and your baby are getting to know each other. You're learning what the different cries mean and how to deal with them. These are the beginnings of a personality. Your baby is learning your touch and your smell and your voice. This is the time when you bond. Fathers, just so we're clear, you need to bond just as much as the mother. This is your baby, too."

She went on to talk about how babies bond and the importance of the connection, but Dev wasn't listening. He'd never bonded with Jimmy. Not in a parental way. Is that what had gone wrong? A lack of bonding on his part?

He'd never thought about emotionally connecting. After their mother died and their father took off, Dev had been concerned about duty and responsibility and doing the right thing. He'd been dealing with his own pain but he'd pushed it aside because he'd wanted to be there for Jimmy, but also to guide him onto the right path.

Right. Instead of illuminating the road to success, Dev had caused a crash and burn—first figuratively, then literally.

"There should be more rules," he said later, when they were in the car driving home.

"Like a checklist?" Noelle asked.

"Exactly. It's day thirty of your baby's life. Here are all the things you need to do."

She laughed. "Dev, it can't be like that. We're talking about people, not an assembly line. Everyone is different."

"Why do they have to be? Rules would help. It's just the word you object to. What if I said 'guidelines'?"

"I'm not sure it makes a difference. Besides, we're going to have a long time before we have to worry about anything but midnight feedings and changing diapers." She touched her stomach. "I'm barely showing."

She wasn't taking this seriously, but then she didn't have his track record.

"I want more information," he said. "When we get home, I want to go online and see what I can find out."

"But it's late," she said. "I'm tired."

"You go to bed. I'll be along in a while."

Her silence told him she wasn't happy with his decision. He thought about explaining, but took the coward's way out and didn't.

He couldn't do anything to help Jimmy, but with a little luck and a lot of determination, he could keep history from repeating itself with Jimmy's child.

Noelle had been looking forward to the Sunday picnic at her parents' house all week. The day was sunny and warm and she'd brought two kinds of salad.

Everything had changed in the past couple of weeks. She wanted to share the information with her mom, but knew that was impossible. Not without first revealing the real reason she'd married Dev, and Noelle wasn't ready to do that yet. Or maybe ever.

"We're here," she called as they walked through the empty house and out into the backyard. "Hi!"

Noelle looked out at the crowd. Her parents were there, of course, along with a couple of neighbors. Her sisters had dates instead of girlfriends, except for Tiffany, who sat on a lounge chair by the pool, reading.

"You made it," her mother said, crossing the patio and kissing them both, then taking the salad bowl from Dev. "Bob is dying for another guy to talk to. Please go rescue him."

"I will. Thanks."

Dev smiled at Noelle, then walked over to her father. The two men shook hands.

"How are you?" her mother asked, linking

arms with her and leading her into the kitchen. "I'm still getting used to having you gone."

"I know," Noelle said as she set her bowl on the counter. "I'm still getting used to living somewhere else."

Her mother opened the refrigerator and made room. "Hmmm, I might buy that, if you weren't so happy. I swear, Noelle, I've never seen you look so…" She straightened and studied her daughter. "Content."

"I'm happy," Noelle said honestly, knowing she'd felt things for Dev she'd never felt before. "I love my life."

"Then I'm happy, too. I'll admit I was a little nervous when you ran off and got married. It was so unlike you."

"I know, Mom. I'm sorry. I didn't mean to hurt you or Dad."

"We weren't hurt. Just surprised. But it's worked out for the best and that's all I could hope for."

Tiffany walked into the kitchen. "I'm bored,"

she announced with all the pain inherent in a moody fifteen-year-old.

"I told you to invite some friends," her mother said.

"I hate that we have to talk about how something happened in our week that changed us. It's stupid." She sighed heavily. "Why do there have to be so many rules?"

Noelle had always felt she and her sisters stood against their parents, but suddenly she found herself on the other side of things. "The rules are good," she said. "They give you boundaries. Trust me, rules are better than no rules."

Tiffany rolled her eyes. "What do you know? You got married and left. You don't have any rules anymore. You can do anything you want. I want that. I want people to stop telling me what to do all the time!"

With that, she stalked out of the kitchen and let the back door slam behind her.

Noelle winced. "Tell me I wasn't that bad."

"Most teenagers are a challenge, in their own way. She'll get through it."

Noelle watched Tiffany walk around the pool and flop down in a chair. "I remember feeling lost and confused about the world when I was her age. It wasn't fun."

Her gaze strayed to where Dev stood talking to her father. At the sight of him, she felt her heartbeat increase. The need to move close, to touch him and kiss him nearly overwhelmed her. But it was more than that. She also wanted to hear his voice and see him smile at her. Life was better when he was with her.

Beside her, her mother sighed. "I remember those days."

Noelle glanced at her. "Being fifteen?"

Her mother smiled. "Being in love and newly married. I couldn't take my eyes off of your dad. Every day was magic and there weren't enough hours for us to express our feelings. What a wonderful time. I wouldn't want to live through being a teenager again, but I wouldn't mind revisiting that romantic intensity for a few days."

Noelle felt herself flush. "We're, um… It's just…"

Her mother laughed. "You don't have to explain it to me. I know exactly what you're thinking."

Noelle doubted that. She and Dev weren't in love the way her mother thought. They were just…

What? What were they? Married, of course. Having a baby together. Living in the same house, caring about each other, building a life. It certainly looked like a strong, healthy relationship. They had respect, mutual affection, attraction.

Her gaze returned to Dev. Whatever they had felt wonderful.

"Noelle, did you mention the medical bills to Dev?"

She blinked and turned her attention to the question. "What? Oh, my bills? I don't think so." She remembered one of their earlier conversations, where she'd confessed she would marry him and had explained the reasons why. That she didn't want to financially burden her family.

She grimaced. "Wait. I did mention them. Should I not have said anything?"

Her mother shrugged. "I can't decide. They've been paid. Anonymously, of course. At first I though it was someone in the congregations, but we know who all the large contributors are and they generally want us to know they're giving. Plus, this is a personal matter and no one knew. Which made it a mystery. Then I thought of Dev."

"He never said anything," Noelle admitted, not sure how to react to the information. "I don't know if it was him."

"There isn't anyone else with both the information and the money."

Had he done that for her? Helped out her family without expecting anything in return? Her chest tightened slightly and she felt all warm and gooey inside.

"I both appreciate the act and respect his desire for privacy," her mother said. "I like that he didn't feel the need to brag about what he'd done. You've chosen well, Noelle. Dev is a good man."

She looked back at the man she'd married. "Yes, he is."

Summer's boyfriend droned on endlessly about the advantages of dual exhaust in his car. Noelle stretched out in the sun and ignored the conversation, even when Dev joined in on the pitfalls of retrofitting something like that on an older car.

Tiffany sat by Noelle's feet on the lounge chair.

"So what's it like being married?" her baby sister asked. "Do you like being on your own?"

Noelle opened her eyes. "I do. I know you think there aren't any rules, but there also isn't anyone else to do the work. Chores don't get split four ways anymore." She didn't mention the cleaning service Dev employed. They came every week and took care of all the big jobs, such as floors, the kitchen, the bathrooms and windows.

Tiffany sniffed. "Chores don't get split four

ways here, now, either. With you gone, they're only split three ways. And when Lily goes to college, it's just going to be Summer and me. It's not fair."

"You think Mom should do everything?" Noelle asked.

Tiffany glared at her. "I knew you'd say something like that. No, I don't think Mom should do everything, but I shouldn't, either. You didn't have to. I hate being the youngest. Everyone is leaving me behind."

Noelle hadn't thought of things from that perspective. "You know I still love you."

Tiffany rolled her eyes. "Yes, and yuck. I'm not talking about that. It's just with you gone and Lily gone, there will be too much attention on Summer and me. Summer's older and she can drive, which means it's just me. I hate that. They're starting to ask questions. Where am I going? Who's going to be there?"

Noelle held in a smile. "They've always done that."

"Yeah, but now they're *listening* to the answers. I have their attention and I don't like it."

Noelle glanced up and saw Dev listening in on the conversation. His combination of half smile and shoulder shrug told her he didn't know what to make of this, either.

"Would you rather they didn't care?" Noelle asked.

"Maybe. Sometimes. It's just all wrong. It's like my name."

"What's wrong with your name?"

"It's stupid." Tiffany rolled her eyes. "Do you know how many other girls have my name? It's a joke. Last year there were three Tiffanys in my geometry class and two different ones in my English class. This guy, David, says he's never going to date a girl named Tiffany because no one will know who he's talking about."

"Then David's an idiot."

"Maybe, but he's really cute."

"So you like him."

Tiffany sighed. "Maybe. But he's not going to be interested in me."

"I wouldn't let the name thing get you down. Boys have a way of changing their mind about things like that."

"Maybe. Or maybe he'll like a different Tiffany." She looked at Dev, then back at Noelle. "He's nice, you know. Better than Summer's stupid boyfriend who only talks about cars."

Noelle looked at her husband and smiled. "He's very nice."

They arrived home late and tired. "You were great with my family," Noelle said as Dev followed her inside. "Tiffany was in a mood today."

"She's a teenager. It happens."

She smiled at him over her shoulder. "Still, all that girl-talk. You were very patient and I appreciate it."

"I didn't mind. I like your family."

"They like you, too. My mom said…"

Noelle's voice trailed off as she stared at him. He was handsome, she thought absently, but that wasn't important. What mattered was the man inside. How he treated her and everyone else in his life. How he was honorable and kind and caring and gentle, yet the strongest man she knew.

She trusted him—not just with herself, but with her child. She trusted him with her heart.

"I love you," she said without meaning to. The words just popped out.

Dev's expression froze.

"I love you," she repeated. She braced herself for a rush of humiliation or regret, but there was only a second of rightness.

She grinned. "Wow. That came from nowhere. I know that's not part of our agreement, but there we are. You're amazing, Dev. I don't know why you're not already married with a bunch of kids. Maybe I got lucky. Whatever the reasons, we're together and I love you."

Until that moment, she'd wondered how she would know what love felt like. Now she knew—she was as certain about her feelings as she had ever been about anything in her life.

He stared at her as if she'd become a stranger. "You can't."

Not exactly the response she would have picked, she thought, trying not to give in to sudden fear. "Well, I do."

"Noelle, stop it. I don't want to talk about this." He took several steps back. "You don't know what you're saying. It's the sex."

"It's more than that," she said, annoyance taking the place of fear. "You don't get to dictate my feelings."

Dev didn't know what kind of game Noelle was playing, but he had to get her to stop. This was not supposed to happen.

"We had a deal," he told her, knowing it was a completely stupid thing to say.

"I broke the rules. Sorry."

It was more than the rules, he thought grimly. There were reasons.

She couldn't love him. People didn't love him.

They wanted him like his women, or hated him like Jimmy, or left him like his parents, but they didn't love him.

He walked around her and left the kitchen. She caught up with him in the hallway.

"You can't pretend this didn't happen," she said as she grabbed his arms. "You can't make my words go away."

"I can try."

"Doesn't it mean anything to you?"

He didn't want to look at her, but he couldn't help himself. He stared into her eyes, into that uncomfortable mixture of pain and hope and knew he'd made a fundamental mistake where she was concerned. Noelle was so damn together, he'd forgotten she wasn't used to playing his kind of game. The one where no one got involved. No one got hurt.

"It means you don't really know me," he said quietly. "If you did, you could never claim to love me."

"There's no *claiming,*" she snapped. "I mean

it. I know what I'm talking about. And I do know you. You're good and kind and smart and caring. You're everything I've ever wanted in a man."

Her words cut him down to the bone. There wasn't blood, but there should have been. Gallons of it. Maybe then, if he shed enough out of guilt, he could make it all right.

"You don't understand," he told her. "I'm not that man. I've screwed up everything important. Everything. My father left because of me. He told me himself. He wanted to go away so I wouldn't be like him. I didn't know what he meant so I didn't know what to change. And Jimmy." He closed his eyes, which only made things worse. Suddenly he could see his kid brother and hear every word of their last, angry conversation.

"Jimmy was the most important person in my life," he said, staring at her. "I was determined to be the best brother, best parent, best everything for him. But it didn't work. Nothing helped. I couldn't get him to care about school or college or getting a job. He wouldn't go to class in high school, he partied, he ran with some pretty bad kids. He got kicked out his junior year. Did he tell you that? Did he tell you he'd tried to set the gym on fire?"

Noelle stared at him, her eyes wide. She slowly shook her head.

"Obviously he never graduated. I hounded him until he got his GED. When that arrived, he told me he was done with me. Not that he moved out—that would have meant taking responsibility for paying bills and he didn't want that." He drew in a breath. "Do you know why you met him at the company? Do you know what he was doing there?"

She shook her head again. "I thought he was working."

"Working." Dev tried to laugh, but there was nothing funny about the situation. "I guess you could call it that. He was stealing parts and selling them on the street. The specialized airplane parts weren't that useful to him, but we have a lot of components that would work with most types of engines. I caught him myself and he wasn't even sorry."

Noelle drew in a breath, but didn't speak.

Dev continued. "I'd had it with him. There had been too many chances, so many screw-ups. I didn't care. Honest to God, in that moment, I hated my brother. I told him he had two choices. He could join the military and grow up, or I would have him arrested and prosecuted. The army or jail. Those were his choices."

Dev shook his head as he tried not to remember the fight he'd had with his brother, the names they'd called each other. Jimmy had said he would never forgive Dev and Dev had said, "Right back at you." They'd nearly punched each other.

"You know what he chose," Dev told her. "That's why he enlisted. He told me where they were sending him and I said it was a good thing. He would have to grow up over there. Learn about responsibility. Quit being such a spoiled little shit. Instead he got dead."

Dev looked at her. "That's what I did, Noelle. I took the easy way out with Jimmy, and because of that, he's dead. There's nothing I can do to change that, no matter how much I want to. I have to live with the consequences of my actions for the rest of my life. I failed my brother. Worse, I killed him. So you might want to think twice about claiming to be in love with someone like me."

Chapter Ten

Dev walked out of the kitchen. Noelle heard the door to the garage close behind him, then the sound of his car starting.

He was leaving. That shocked her nearly as much as what he'd told her. How could he dump all that on her and then leave?

She stood in the silence for several minutes, then slowly turned off lights and made her way to the bedroom she shared with the man she'd married. A thousand different thoughts flowed through her brain. She didn't know what to think, what to believe. The only thing she completely understood was that Dev was out of reach in ways she couldn't begin to understand.

He never came home the whole night. Noelle tried to sleep, but couldn't, and was up and prowling restlessly before dawn. She made a large pot of coffee in anticipation of his arrival, which never happened, then turned it off before she left for school.

As she drove to the campus, she once again went over what he'd told her. She'd known Jimmy well enough to see how he could easily make someone like Dev completely crazy. Jimmy had been on a slick, steep road to destruction and, one way or another, he was going to have to pay for that.

But not with his life, she thought sadly as she parked and collected her books. No one should have to pay that high a price. And what about Dev, left behind, with only his guilt to keep him company?

She could almost understand why he wouldn't

let the past go. It was too painful and so easy for him to blame himself, which meant he was a man on a mission—that he had to somehow make up for what he'd done. That explained his nearly obsessive desire to be a part of Jimmy's child's life and why he'd insisted on marriage. But where did that leave her? Was she any part of his plan, or just the vessel who carried his brother's unborn child? Had she fallen in love with a man who didn't see her as a real person?

Late that afternoon, she still didn't have any answer. Not sure if she would even see Dev again, she couldn't decide if she should cook dinner or not. Talk about a stupid concern if her husband had walked out on her. But it was easier to focus on that, than the fact she might never see him again. She told herself she had to eat something. She would make enough for two and if he didn't come home, she would have the rest for lunch the next day.

Shortly after five she heard the garage door open. Her heart leapt in her chest, but she forced herself not to react when he walked into the kitchen. She finished chopping the bell pepper, then wiped her hands on a towel and turned to face him.

He looked awful. There were dark shadows under his eyes and a heaviness to his step. She doubted he'd slept, although he'd obviously showered and changed clothes somewhere. She remembered the fabulous bathroom attached to his office, which was, ironically, the place where all this started. If he hadn't caught her coming out of his office that morning, he wouldn't have known about the baby.

She would have told him eventually, she thought, what with him being Jimmy's only relative, but by then she would have gone to her parents and who knows what would have happened. She doubted they would be married right now.

He shrugged out of his suit jacket and slung it on the counter. "I'm sorry," he said. "I shouldn't have left like that. I had no right to worry you.

I thought about calling, but by the time it occurred to me, it was about three in the morning and I hoped you would be asleep."

"I wasn't," she said softly, trying not to show how relieved she felt to see him.

He ran his hand through his hair. "Walking out isn't my normal solution to an argument," he admitted. "I don't know what happened."

"It's an emotional topic."

"Still no excuse," he muttered. "It won't happen again."

She wanted to ask why. Did he mean he would handle things better in the future or that they wouldn't be in a position to have fights because they wouldn't be together?

She turned off the burners she'd lit on the stove and moved both the pan and the pot to the side.

"We need to talk about this," she said. "About Jimmy."

He stiffened. "No, we don't."

"You can't dump something like that on me and then refuse to discuss it again. It's too important. You're in pain, Dev. I understand why you miss him, but you're not responsible for his death. You didn't make him screw up his life, you didn't make him steal and you didn't pull the trigger on the gun that killed him."

"I will not discuss this with you."

His voice was ice and she shivered from the cold.

"Dev…"

"I like you and respect you," he said firmly, "but this topic is off-limits. I also want to be clear about a few other things. As far as I'm concerned, the initial rules are still in place. In two years, this marriage ends."

She felt as if he'd slapped her. "We've moved past that already."

"No, we haven't. Sleeping together doesn't change anything. I *will* walk away in two years." He drew in a breath. "I understand if you have to think about all this and even if you want me to move out while you consider it."

His tone softened, but his words still cut her.

Sleeping together? Is that what he thought they were doing? For her, it was much more than that.

She looked at him and wondered what he wasn't saying. Was he trying to get her to back away? She knew he enjoyed their lovemaking, so she didn't think he wanted that to end. So what was this about? Did he need her at arm's length so he wouldn't start to care? Or was that just wishful thinking on her part?

She wanted to believe that he was afraid of falling in love with her, but what proof did she have? Except for his overzealous guilt about Jimmy, Dev seemed like a regular guy. Why would he be afraid of loving anyone? He was certainly committed to Jimmy's child.

Was he afraid *she* would leave, so he was protecting himself, or was that even more wishful thinking?

"You don't need to leave," she said slowly. "If anyone were to leave, it would be me."

She thought he tensed, but she wasn't sure.

"Are you leaving?" he asked.

"No. I'm your wife and I want to stay with you."

"In my bed?" he asked bluntly. "Are you willing to sleep with me, knowing there's a time limit?"

He was trying to push her away, but why? Would it make him feel better or worse to have her agree to his terms?

There was no way for her to know and she believed if she asked, he would avoid the question. Which meant she could only worry about herself and what she wanted.

"I still love you," she said. "My feelings aren't up for grabs, nor can you dictate or legislate them. My question for you is can *you* handle that? Can you live in this house with me, knowing how I feel?"

His dark eyes gave nothing away. "In two years, it's over."

He had the final power in that, she thought sadly. He couldn't make her stop loving him and she couldn't make him care about her. In the end, if he didn't want her anymore, she would go.

"You're my husband and I'm committed to

this relationship," she told him. "For as long as we're together, I will share everything I have with you, including my heart and my body."

"Then you're staying."

She nodded.

"Good." He grabbed his jacket. "I'll go get changed."

"Dinner's in about thirty minutes."

He nodded and left. Noelle stared after him and wondered if he recognized that nothing had been resolved. They'd entered into an uneasy peace for the moment, but the final outcome was anyone's guess.

A week later Noelle found herself continuing to live in a state of uncertainty. While she and Dev occupied the same house, they weren't the loving, happy couple they'd been before she'd confessed her feelings and he'd told her about Jimmy.

She and Dev spoke about everything that wasn't important, shared physical space without touching and were painfully polite. At night they each claimed their side of the large bed, with neither making a move toward the other.

In truth, she missed him. She missed laughing with him and touching him. She missed making love and feeling a part of something, but with no idea how to fix the problem, she didn't know how to change things. Talking hadn't gotten them anywhere and while she was fairly confident that if she reached for him he wouldn't reject her, she wasn't sure she was ready to make the first move.

For once, her lack of experience was a handicap. She didn't know how to handle the situation and she was too embarrassed to discuss it with Rachel and Crissy. As far as her friends were concerned, everything was perfect in the Hunter household.

Noelle had never lived a lie before and she didn't like living one now. But how to change things? Did they each need a good knock over the head?

By the time she drove into the driveway after her study group, she didn't have any answers.

But she was surprised to see Dev's car in the garage. It was only three in the afternoon. What was he doing home?

"Dev?" she called as she walked into the kitchen.

She saw him standing in the family room, along with Tiffany and what looked like enough luggage for an entire graduating class.

Her sister took one look at her and burst into tears. Noelle instinctively held out her arms. Tiffany rushed to her and hung on tight.

"Your mother called," Dev said as she patted her sister's back. "When you didn't pick up here, she called me at work."

Tiffany stepped back. "I hate my life. I hate it so much. I hate living at home. Mom and Dad are so awful. I don't want to live with them anymore. I want to come live with you."

Because they needed one more thing, Noelle thought, trying to see the humor in the situation and failing.

"I'll be good," Tiffany said, wiping the tears

from her eyes. "I promise. It's just they don't understand anything. Please, Noelle, don't make me go back."

Dev motioned for her to follow him down the hall.

"Wait here," Noelle told her sister, then followed him into their bedroom. "I can't believe this," she said when he'd shut the door.

"It's a surprise," he admitted. "Your mom called and said Tiffany was running away. Apparently a friend picked her up. Your mom said if we could stand to have her stay for a few days, it would be a big help. She thinks Tiffany needs a dose of reality."

"She needs more than that," Noelle muttered, then waited for Dev to announce that there was no way he was letting her kid sister move in with them. Only he didn't.

"Aren't you upset?" she asked.

He shrugged. "I'm gone most of the time. She's your sister and you're the one who would be home with her. It's your call."

She blinked. Never would she have guessed *those* words would come out of his mouth. Something was wrong, but she couldn't figure out what.

Dev waited while Noelle considered her options. What he wasn't about to admit was that he saw Tiffany as an unexpected distraction. Things had been tense between Noelle and him. A third person might improve the situation, or at least keep them so busy that they'd forget to be painfully polite all the time.

He knew he'd hurt her and he hated that. He'd been so damn careful to spell out all the rules so that wouldn't happen, only he'd forgotten to address the possibility of feelings and sexual desire.

He'd known making love with Noelle was a mistake. The shared intimacy had convinced her she had feelings for him. He didn't consider that her feelings might be real. How could she know what he'd done and still care about him? Still, he'd upset her and caused her pain, when all she'd done was surprise him in the best way possible, over and over again.

"If you don't mind, then let's tell Tiffany she can stay," Noelle said. "Although it's not going to be the cushy vacation she's expecting." She squared her shoulders. "Okay, I'm ready."

They returned to the family room. Tiffany stood anxiously by her piles of luggage. "What?" the teenager asked. "Noelle, you have to let me live here."

Noelle stared at her. "You can stay."

Tiffany shrieked and jumped in the air. "Really? That's so great! I'm going to be so incredibly fun to have around, you'll beg me never to leave. Can I live in the pool house? It looks fabulous."

"It is, but you'll be in the house, staying in the guest room."

The one Noelle had recently vacated, Dev thought, knowing this would be a lot more awkward if she hadn't already moved in with him.

"There is also a condition," Noelle continued.

"I'll do anything," Tiffany promised.

Noelle didn't look convinced. "Okay—the condition is you follow my rules."

Tiffany shoved her long, blond hair off her shoulders and sighed heavily. "What rules?"

Noelle smiled. "You'll like them. Some of them will even be familiar. One, you will have a list of chores to be completed on a daily basis. Two, you will have a curfew and be home by nine."

"Nine?" Tiffany shrieked. "Nine at night?"

"Three," Noelle continued, ignoring her. "No boys in the house. Not ever, not for five minutes. None. Zero. Girlfriends are allowed, but only when one of us is home. Girlfriends will vacate the house by nine unless they are staying for a preapproved sleepover. Four, you will not go into the pool when you are home alone. Five, you will play your music at a reasonable volume and we determine what is reasonable." She paused. "That's all I can think of for now, but there may be more later. If you violate any of these, I'll pack your stuff myself and toss you out. Is that clear?"

Tiffany stared at her sister as if she'd never

seen her before. "You're worse than Mom," she breathed, then turned to Dev. "Tell her she's being unfair."

Dev held up both hands. "This is between the two of you. Leave me out of it."

On the one hand, he thought Noelle's rules were strict, but on the other, he understood her plan. She was trying to make Tiffany see that running away didn't solve anything. A lesson he obviously needed to learn himself, based on how he'd acted after their big fight.

"Dev works and I'm taking classes," Noelle said firmly. "Everyone in this house has responsibilities and that includes you, kid. So what do you say?"

Tiffany sighed. For a second, Dev thought she was going to balk, but she nodded slowly. "Okay. Fine. I'll follow the rules."

"Good. I'll take you to day care every morning and pick you up at five."

He frowned. "Tiffany's in day care?" She seemed kind of old.

Tiffany giggled. "I don't go. I help. Through the church. Teenagers who are too young to get jobs and stuff volunteer. We don't get paid, but we will get a nice reference, which helps us when we want to get real jobs."

That made sense. He picked up several of the suitcases. "I'll carry these back." He looked at Noelle. "The bigger of the two rooms." Meaning the one she'd occupied.

She nodded. "Take a bag, Tiffany. You're not in a hotel."

Her sister sighed. "Yes, ma'am."

She slung a couple of totes over her shoulder and followed him down the hall.

"Here's the room," Dev said, pushing open the door. "Bathroom is next door."

Tiffany dropped her bags and flung herself onto the bed. "It's really nice. At home I share with Summer. Lily shared with Noelle. With Lily going off to college, Summer's getting her room and I'll have Lily with me when she's back from school. But our room isn't nearly as cool as this."

She sat up. "Noelle is really bossy. She likes to take charge and be responsible. Boys don't like that in a girl. Doesn't it make you crazy?"

He set down the suitcases. "No. But then I'm not a boy and your sister is my wife."

Tiffany's eyes widened. "Wow. So you like her?"

He smiled. "Yes. Very much. I think Noelle is terrific and beautiful."

Tiffany flopped back on the bed. "I want someone to think I'm terrific. Does that mean I have to act that way?"

"Pretty much."

Later, when Tiffany was busy unpacking what appeared to be everything she'd ever owned, Dev walked into the master bedroom and found Noelle curled up in the window seat.

"Are you sure about this?" he asked.

She turned to face him and he saw tears on her cheeks. Panic seized him.

"What happened?" he demanded as he crossed the room. "Noelle, what's wrong?"

She shook her head. "I'm fine," she whispered.

Like he believed that. "Then why are you crying?" He sat next to her and reached for her hand, but stopped himself.

She drew in a breath. "I heard you talking to Tiffany. I heard what you said. How can you tell her I'm terrific and tell me that in two years you'll walk away without looking back?"

Damn. "The two statements have nothing in common."

"I disagree. Either you feel something for me or you don't."

This time he did capture her hand and rubbed his fingers against hers. "I respect you and admire you. I want you. But I will not love you and you shouldn't love me."

More tears trickled down her cheeks. Her eyes were the color of a midnight sky and he could feel her pain. "Why? It's not just because of Jimmy. It can't be. What else is there?"

He didn't know how to explain. There were so many reasons and his need to protect Noelle was powerful and strong. He'd watched his mother fade away from a broken heart when his father had refused to care for her. He didn't want that to happen to Noelle.

No doubt she would tell him that the solution was for him to love her, but he couldn't. He had loved his parents and they had both left him. He'd loved Jimmy and had ended up destroying his brother. Love was dangerous and ended in loss.

"When this is over, you'll find someone else," he said quietly. "Someone willing to give you his whole heart."

She snatched back her hand. "Do you think I want someone else? I haven't given my heart lightly. Love just is, Dev, whether you want it or not. You can't command it or explain it. Has it occurred to you that I might love you forever?"

He stood and stared at her. "Don't," he said hoarsely, knowing he would never have wanted that for her. "Don't love me, Noelle. I'm not worth it."

She looked at him sadly. "Apparently, neither am I."

* * *

Saturday morning Dev pretended to work in his home office, but in truth he did little more than stare at a computer screen. From outside came the screams of laughter as six fifteen-year-old girls and Noelle's other sisters played in the pool.

Part of him wanted to join Noelle and part of him wanted to run for the hills. Being around her had grown more difficult in the past few days.

She never said anything reproachful, never yelled or pouted. But he felt her gaze on him and knew she watched and wondered why he couldn't simply love her back. She didn't understand what she asked. She didn't know how impossible everything had become.

It was only two years, he reminded himself. Surely they could survive that long. Then she would be free to leave and start over.

Except what if she were right? What if she did only ever love him?

He rose and walked out into the family room. From there he could see the backyard and the pool. Noelle sat by the water. Did she avoid the play because she wasn't in the mood or was she afraid a bathing suit would give away her secret?

She'd lied to everyone she'd ever loved because of him, he thought grimly. She'd wanted to go to her parents and tell them the truth and he'd wanted to take control. He'd known that he had to be a part of the baby's life, so that he could atone for what he'd done to Jimmy. The decision had seemed right at the time, but now…he wasn't so sure.

The doorbell rang. He hurried toward the front of the house, grateful for the distraction. But when he opened the door, he knew there was always a price for everything.

A man stood on the doorstep. It had been fourteen years, but despite the increase in gray hair and wrinkles, Dev recognized him.

His father offered him a tentative smile. "Hello, son."

Chapter Eleven

Noelle walked into the house and found Dev facing down a handsome older man. There was enough tension in the room to strangle an elephant. Seeing as Dev was an experienced executive and used to dealing with lots of difficult people, she was going to go out on a limb and say the guy wasn't selling magazine subscriptions.

"Noelle," Dev said between clenched teeth. "I'd like you to meet Jackson Hunter. My father."

Father? Noelle stared at the older man. Father as in the guy who ran out on his two sons days after their mother died? Father as in the guy who told Dev he had to leave to keep his oldest son from turning out just like him?

"Mr. Hunter," Noelle said, her tone icy. "This is unexpected."

The older man smiled at her. "I know, my dear. You have every right to be angry with me. I just hope you'll understand when an old man comes home to make amends with his only family."

Noelle opened her mouth and closed it. Dev *was* his only family, now that Jimmy was gone. Except for the baby. Which mean Jackson was her baby's grandfather.

She looked into Jackson's brown eyes and saw a lifetime of pain there. "It's been a long time," she said.

"Too long. I wanted to come back before, but I didn't know how."

"A plane would be a conventional way of traveling," Dev said flatly. "A car, if you're in the area. A boat could work, to the coast, of course."

Jackson Hunter flinched.

Dev didn't seem to notice. "If you'll excuse me, I have work to do," he said, then left.

Noelle thought about calling him back, but had no idea what to say. These days, she and Dev were barely speaking.

"It's all right," his father said. "I wasn't a very good father while I was around and leaving didn't improve my status."

"Dev said you told him you left so he wouldn't turn out like you," she said before she could stop herself.

Jackson frowned. "Did I?" He considered the statement. "I don't think so. It's true I didn't want him to be a failure. I could see so much potential in him. I thought if I were out of the way, he could reach that potential. It was my father's idea. He would take the boys and I…" The old man shrugged. "It was a long time ago. I took the easy way out. Later, I wondered if I should have stayed. But there's no going back now, is there?"

Noelle didn't know what to say. This was not

how Dev told the story and since he had no reason to lie, she could only assume he'd repeated what he'd heard. His father's leaving had been his grandfather's idea?

"Dev's all I have left," Jackson continued. "I came as soon as I heard about Jimmy."

Noelle instinctively touched her stomach. There was more than Dev, but this wasn't the time to get into that.

"I'm sorry for your loss," she said automatically.

"Did you know him?" Jackson asked hopefully. "He was so young when I left. What was he like?"

She thought about all she knew about Jimmy and decided that there was no reason for his father to have all the details. "He was funny and charming and far too young to die," she said quietly. "Even in the service of his country."

Jackson seemed to age right before her eyes. "My baby boy is gone." His voice shook as he spoke. Then he cleared his throat and straightened. "I've bothered you enough. I'll be leaving now."

"You can't go," Noelle said impulsively. "Please, stay. My fifteen-year-old sister has just run away from home and settled here, so you'll have to put up with shrieking girls and loud music. But we have a pool house that is comfortable and a little away from all the action. Let me show you."

Thirty minutes later Jackson Hunter had carried his two suitcases into the pool house and changed into worn swim trunks and a T-shirt. He joined the girls by the pool where he stunned them all by knowing the words to the song blaring from the radio.

"He's not staying," Dev said, coming up to stand beside her in the kitchen as she prepared sandwiches for lunch.

"He's your father."

"That's a technicality."

"He's your family. He's old and he's here to make amends."

"That's not possible."

She looked at Dev. "Sometimes you are so pigheaded, I just want to shake you. Have you ever considered there are things you don't know that might change everything?" She hesitated, not sure if she should share what she'd been told, then figured it couldn't make things worse. "Your father left because he believed you had a future," she said, then explained what Jackson had told her.

"It wasn't my grandfather's idea," he said heatedly, when she'd finished.

"Why would your father lie?"

"To make himself look better."

"Calling himself a failure makes him look really good, right?"

Dev frowned. "He wasn't a failure. He worked at the company until he left. He provided for us. He didn't fail."

"Funny how he thinks he did. And that's before he walked out on his two kids. Imagine how he feels now."

He narrowed his gaze. "Don't get in the middle of this, Noelle."

"I'll do my best not to," she said. "In return, maybe you could keep an open mind."

Dev swore. "He's been here less than an hour and he's getting to you. Let's cut to the chase. The man walked out on his two children right after their mother died. How am I supposed to forgive that?"

"I don't know," she told him. "Maybe you start by listening."

The following Saturday afternoon Dev found himself invaded by yet more of Tiffany's friends. There was a chick-flick movie fest going on in the family room and way too much sugar happening in the kitchen. Noelle was at her study group and he couldn't seem to concentrate on the work he'd brought home.

If it had been Jimmy instead of Tiffany, he would have ordered everyone out and enjoyed the subsequent silence. But as his relationship with his brother had gone so badly, he decided to ignore his instincts. Which left him restless, with nowhere to go.

As he couldn't stand one more shriek of laughter or the off-tone music from an erupting cell phone, he walked outside, only to be faced by the pool house. His father had been in residence nearly a week and Dev had managed to avoid the man completely. Maybe it was time to change that.

But when he approached the pool house he was surprised to see the door open and Bob, Noelle's father, sitting on the sofa.

"Dev," Bob said, spotting him before he could escape. "We were just talking about you."

"I'll bet," Dev said, then stepped inside. "Sir."

He shook hands with his father-in-law and nodded at his own father.

"Noelle called me a couple of days ago and asked me to stop by," Bob said. "She seemed to think I might have some insight."

Dev wasn't sure how he felt about that. Noelle

hadn't discussed contacting her father with him, but then they weren't having all that many conversations these days.

"Son." His father stood and motioned to the small refrigerator in the corner of what was basically a game room/studio apartment. "Can I get you something to drink?"

Several sofas and a large-screen TV dominated the space. There was a Murphy bed against one wall, a kitchenette and a full bathroom.

"I'm good," Dev said, wishing he'd never come out here. Now there was no way to politely escape. He sat across from his father, on the same sofa as Bob.

"Your dad was just telling me about his travels," Bob said easily. "He spent a lot of time in the South Pacific."

"Is that where you went?" Dev asked, not really interested in the details.

"Mostly. I worked in hotels. Ran tours, managed a bar for a while. I moved around a lot. I was never very good at staying in one place."

He made the statement deliberately, as if daring Dev to comment. Dev didn't respond.

Jackson continued, "I realized I was looking for roots, when I'd already left them behind."

Dev fought against feeling any emotion, even when a surge of anger swept through him. Leaving roots behind? Is that how his father characterized leaving two children right after their mother had died?

Bob picked up his can of soda. "A lot of people go looking for what they've already had and lost."

Jackson looked at Dev. "I'm sorry I left, son. I know the words won't mean much, but I'm speaking from the heart. You and Jimmy were…"

Jimmy! Dev stiffened. "You know what happened to Jimmy?"

"I heard," his father told him. "Not through the military, of course. You were his next of kin. But I kept in touch with a few friends here and there and they got me word."

Dev had never felt so torn in his life. Part of him ached with the realization that a man had lost a son, while the rest of him hated Jackson Hunter for keeping in touch with his friends but not his boys.

"There you are," Noelle said from the door of the pool house. "I came home to a houseful of teenagers and not another adult in sight. It was a little scary."

"You're back," Dev said as he jumped to his feet. He'd never been so grateful for an interruption before in his life.

He crossed to her and pulled her close, then kissed her. "I missed you."

She smiled quizzically. "I guess you did. I'll have to go away more so I can get greetings like this again. Hi, Dad. Jackson. How's it going?"

"Good. I should probably be heading home in a few minutes. Your mother's making a pot roast tonight and I never miss one of those."

"I remember." Noelle wrinkled her nose. "I should do a head count for dinner, myself."

"Want some help?" Dev asked.

Her blue eyes seemed to see more than they

should, but he didn't care. Anything to get out of this conversation.

"Sure," she said. "Assuming we can be heard over the movie. It's so loud in there. You know, you're allowed to tell them to turn it down. Jackson, want to join us?"

So far his father had avoided meals with the family, but this time, he nodded. "Sure."

"Good." Noelle took Dev's hand and turned toward the house. "Give me a couple of hours to get myself together. Say six?"

"Sounds good."

"Okay. Daddy, come in and say goodbye before you leave."

"Will do."

With that, Dev and Noelle made their way toward the house.

"Are you angry that I asked my dad over?" she asked when they were by the French doors leading inside. Even from out here, he could hear the loud soundtrack on the movie.

"No. Having a third party around is a good idea."

She stared into his eyes. "He's just an old man, Dev. He's not the devil."

"I'm having trouble reconciling the two thoughts. He lost a son. I never got that before and I feel bad for him."

"But?"

"But he admitted he'd kept in touch with friends in the area. Why the hell would he be in contact with them and not us? We're his children. He just walked, Noelle. I don't care whose idea it was. He just walked."

She surprised him by leaning forward and wrapping her arms around him. "I know," she whispered. "I really like him, but then I think about what he did to you and it's awful. I know I said you should reconcile and I still believe that. It's the only way to heal those wounds inside, but it's not going to be easy. I guess we were never promised easy, huh?"

Instead of answering, he bent down and kissed her. Her lips were soft and yielding and she returned the kiss with enough passion to make him resent every person standing between him and some serious private time with the woman in his arms.

"I want you," he breathed when they came up for air.

Her mouth quivered. "You haven't wanted me for a long time."

He rubbed his thumb against her lower lip. "You're wrong. I always want you. I haven't acted on it."

"Why?"

Suddenly he wasn't sure. "Things were complicated."

"They always will be," she told him. "I didn't ask you to stay away."

"Then I won't."

"Good." She looked into the family room and sighed. "I need to go take care of that," she said. "Want to come along for a good screaming?"

"Sure." He didn't care about the screaming, but he was interested in how Noelle would handle the situation.

She walked into the house and paused. The volume was so loud, the walls shook. When she moved forward, she bent down, grabbed the remote and hit the pause button.

All seven girls turned to stare at her.

"Let's be reasonable about the volume," she said into the silence. "Who's staying for dinner?"

Two girls raised their hands.

"I want names and phone numbers," she said. "I'll be calling home to verify it's all right."

"Noelle," Tiffany protested. "Can't we just have fun?"

"Apparently not," her sister said cheerfully. She looked at her watch. "It's nearly four. Everyone not staying to dinner will be gone by five. For the rest of you, dinner is at six, and curfew is at nine."

Tiffany groaned. "You're such a pain."

"I know, and being a pain is the highlight of my day. Everyone understand?"

The other girls nodded. The two staying for

dinner stood and followed Noelle into the kitchen, where Dev knew she would make good on her word and check with their parents. Tiffany's friends who weren't hanging around pulled out cell phones and began to make calls to ask to be picked up.

He walked into the kitchen, where she was dialing the phone.

"When did you get so good at this?" he asked.

"I took a class."

"I'm serious."

"I don't know," she admitted. "I watched my mom handle things. I try to think about what she would have done."

Too bad her mother hadn't been around when he'd been screwing things up with Jimmy. Maybe then his brother wouldn't be dead. Of course, if Jimmy were still alive then he, Dev, wouldn't be married to Noelle. Despite everything, he couldn't actually say he didn't want to be with her. Which meant he was in more trouble than he'd thought.

* * *

Noelle came out of the bathroom that night and found Dev sitting up in bed. Since she'd declared her love for him and he'd walked out, they'd slept in the same room, but he'd made sure they never went to bed at the same time. He always came in after she was asleep and was gone before she got up.

She paused in the doorway. "You're not working late tonight?"

"No."

Did that mean what she thought it meant? Anticipation fluttered inside of her. She loved him and desired him in equal measures. Having things unsettled between them had been painful. She wanted to be in his arms so much, but at the same time, she was afraid. So much of their relationship confused her. Was it right to give herself to him, knowing he didn't return her feelings?

Then he smiled at her. The curve of his lips was both apology and invitation. Her gaze dropped to his bare chest and she wondered if he'd pulled on boxers or if he wore nothing at all.

Maybe walking away was the smart thing to do, but Noelle chose to follow her heart. She walked the few steps to the bed, then climbed between the cool sheets.

Dev reached for her and pulled her against his body.

Naked, she thought as need poured through her. Naked and already hard. How was she supposed to resist that?

"Do you want to do this?" he asked as he gazed into her eyes. "I'll stop if you ask me to."

"Now why would I do a really stupid thing like that?"

He lowered his head and kissed her. She parted and his tongue swept inside, exploring her, arousing her, making her squirm with need.

Her leg brushed against his arousal. She reached down and traced the hard line of his thigh, then slipped between his legs until she could take him in her hand.

Velvet on steel. She'd read that in a book once and had giggled, alone in her room. But now she got the description completely. The skin was so soft, but underneath that thin layer was a hardness that made her ache to be claimed. She wanted to part her legs and demand that he take her right then. Only if she did that, she would miss out on all the good stuff between now and then. It was not an easy decision to make.

He shifted away, leaving her longing to touch him again. Before she could complain, he tugged her nightgown over her head, then pulled down her panties. He bent over her breasts and took one of her nipples in his mouth.

The combination of moist heat and gentle sucking made her arch her back and bite down on a scream. Pleasure exploded with each tug of his mouth. His tongue teased her sensitive flesh until she was willing to offer anything if he just promised not to stop.

He used his hand to caress her other breast, mimicking the acts of his tongue with his fingers. She let herself fall into the sensation. Between her legs heat and moisture competed for dominance. She wanted him there. She wanted him to keep touching her breasts. She wanted everything he could give her and then she wanted to give it all back to him.

He shifted between her legs, then kissed his way down her rib cage and over the small mound that was the only sign of her pregnancy. She knew what he was going to do—he'd done it once before. That intimate kiss that had pushed her so close to losing control.

She'd held back a little, unsure she could give herself up to him while so vulnerable and exposed, and he'd stopped. While he'd brought her to her release with his fingers, and later by being inside of her, she'd wondered what it would have felt like if he'd kept on going.

She parted her legs for him, then closed her eyes in anticipation of his touch.

Her first warning was the soft whisper of air. Then he licked her from bottom to top in one smooth, gentle movement. A shiver of delight rippled through her. She clutched the sheets and arched her head back as he circled that one special spot, moving closer but not touching.

Delicious, she thought as her muscles tensed and the soles of her feet began to burn. Delicious and exciting and so incredible that she wasn't sure how she was going to find the strength to hold back this time.

So maybe she wouldn't. Maybe she would just give in to the whisper touch of his tongue moving back and forth over her swollen center.

Tension filled her. She drew in deeper and deeper breaths. It was as if every cell of her body had all its attention focused on that one spot and what he was doing there.

He moved faster—circling, teasing, sliding across. Everything felt out of her control. She was getting closer. She could feel her muscles clenching as she pushed toward her release. It was so close.

He slipped a finger inside of her. The unexpected action shocked her and she opened her eyes. For a second, she saw the top of his dark head as he pleasured her, then she closed her eyes again, almost embarrassed by what she'd seen.

But the picture of that intimate act stayed with her. The more she thought about it, the more aroused she got. Then he began to move the finger inside of her, sliding it in and out, almost as if he was rubbing her center from underneath while his tongue loved it from above.

She came in a wave of contractions that made her whole body tremble. She could no more have stopped herself than she could have escaped gravity. From head to toe, she experienced wild, intense pleasure that took her breath away.

She wanted to scream her release, but forced herself to hold in her cry. Then, while she was still caught in her release, Dev sat up and plunged into her.

He was thick and hard and filled her until she had no choice but to come again. She needed him, all of him. Without thinking, she grabbed his hips and pulled him to her.

He braced himself and pumped into her over and over again. She parted her thighs more, then wrapped her legs around his hips, doing everything she could think of to pull him all in.

Again and again he filled her, sending more waves crashing through her. It wasn't possible for her body to feel this much, she thought. Maybe she would never stop. Maybe they could go on forever.

But then he gave one last great thrust and her body shattered into such intense release that she knew she had reached the ultimate moment. His body tensed and she felt him let go inside of her.

She opened her eyes and found him watching her. They gazed at each other, naked and exposed, seeing the truth in each of their souls.

They were both breathing hard. Dev started to move, but she held him in place.

"Not yet," she whispered. "I want to stay like this for another second."

He smiled. "Pretty incredible."

"The best."

A muscle cramped in her hip and she had to move. In the logistics of postlovemaking, she started to giggle.

"It was hard not to scream," she whispered. "I had to hold it in so I wouldn't scare my sister."

"I appreciate that," he said as he settled on the mattress next to her and tucked her hair behind her ears. "Having Tiffany walk in would have deflated the moment."

"It also would have led to a lot of questions. I'm glad I was able to control myself."

He kissed her forehead. "I'm glad you weren't." He studied her. "You're amazing. You can handle your family, my father, this house, school and you're incredibly wicked in bed."

"Wicked?" She liked the sound of that. "Only with you, Dev."

The words slipped out and she would have given anything to call them back.

"Noelle, don't," he said.

"I'm not trying to go there. I don't want to spoil this."

"Me, either."

But the words *had* been spoken and there was no calling them back. The mood shifted until she found herself saying, "I still love you. Nothing has changed."

He shifted back onto his side of the bed. "I've told you not to."

"Yeah, that's going to work." She raised herself on one elbow and faced him. "What are you so afraid of?"

"I don't want you getting hurt."

Which sounded very altruistic, but she wasn't sure she believed him. "What more could you possibly want from a wife? What need don't I fulfill?"

It was a dangerous question and an honest answer could emotionally devastate her. Still, she was willing to risk it and hear the truth.

"It's not you," he said slowly. "There's nothing wrong with you. It's me. I can't love you."

She stared at him for a long time and wondered if being told she wasn't pretty enough or smart enough or sensitive enough would have been easier to deal with. This truth cut deep.

"It's not that you can't," she told him. "It's that you won't."

Chapter Twelve

Noelle knocked on her parents' front door. She'd never done that before—she'd always just burst in. But this was different. Now she didn't live here anymore.

Her mother answered, then laughed. "Noelle, you might be all grown-up and married, but you're still my baby girl. You don't have to knock."

Noelle opened her mouth to answer, then shocked herself and probably her mother by bursting into tears.

Five minutes later they were both on the worn

sofa in the small living room. There was a box of tissues in her lap and her mother's arms around her.

"Shh," her mom whispered as they rocked back and forth. "I'm here, honey. I'll always be here. Whatever it is, we can fix it together."

"I m-messed up," Noelle said, her voice breaking with sobs. "I messed up so badly."

"The first few months of any marriage are difficult. You and Dev will get through it. I know it seems impossible now, but in time, things will get better. The most important thing is you love each other."

"We d-don't," Noelle said as she tried to control her tears. "I mean, I love him, but he doesn't…"

Her mother straightened and cupped her face. "Of course he loves you. Why else would he marry you?"

Noelle swallowed, then cleared her throat. "Because he thought it was the right thing to do."

She told her everything. She talked about dating Jimmy and how fast everything had moved. That he'd gone into the army and then been shipped overseas. She glossed over that single night they'd shared, then confessed her pregnancy and how Dev had found out only seconds after she'd seen the truth, herself.

"He took charge," she said as she wiped her face with another tissue. "I'm not saying I don't have responsibility in what happened. Of course I do. It's just I was terrified and he was there, telling me exactly what we should do. He made it sound easy and sensible." She clutched her hands around the damp wad of tissue. "How disappointed are you?"

Her mother smiled. "I'm not disappointed, Noelle. You gave in to a boy in a moment of passion and emotion. It happens. It's happened for thousands of years. Smart girls make impulsive decisions that change their lives forever."

"I thought I loved him," she admitted. "Or maybe I was just trying to convince myself I did to make my actions seem less stupid. But I didn't. I love Dev, only he doesn't want me to.

He says we have a deal and that's the most important thing. Our agreement."

"Tell me about the agreement," her mother said.

Noelle explained the details of what Dev had offered. It was hard to admit she'd taken money for having a child she would have had anyway, but...

She stopped. Instead of being angry and shocked, her mother was smiling.

"What are you so happy about?"

Her mother hugged her. "You're having a baby. My very first grandchild. I was kind of hoping I could be at least forty-five before that happened, but under the circumstances, I'm willing to go with it."

Noelle blinked. "You're happy about the baby?"

"Of course. Noelle, you have no idea how wonderful it is to have children. Your life will change forever, but in the best way possible. How far along are you? When are you due? Have you seen a doctor?"

"Three months, early March and yes, Dev and I have been to a doctor. We've also signed up for parenting classes and we have every book on pregnancy ever published."

They hugged again. "Yay, you," her mother said. "I can't wait to tell your father."

"I'm not sure he'll be as understanding as you've been."

"You might be surprised." Her mother patted her arm. "Okay, where were you? You married Dev because of the baby. You know you could have come to us and told us what was going on."

"I know. I wanted to…" She stared at her lap. "I started to, actually." She explained about the day she'd come home and found her mother crying over the bills and having to leave the church and that she couldn't bring a baby into the house.

"We would have found a way," her mom said.

"I know. But I thought marrying Dev was an easier option. Only now I've fallen in love with him and he doesn't want me to."

"Tell me about that," her mother said.

"I was so scared at first, but he made everything wonderful." She talked about how they got to know each other and how the more they knew, the more there was to like.

"I couldn't believe it was so easy," she admitted. "We mesh. He even likes peanut butter cookies better than chocolate chip, just like me. He wants to be there for the baby. He's kind and responsible and…"

"Incredible in bed."

Noelle felt herself blush. "Mo-om."

"He must be or it would be a lot easier to leave."

"That part of our relationship is fine," she said primly.

Her mother laughed. "My daughter, the prude."

"I'm not a prude. Sex with Dev is amazing, but you're my mother."

"Okay, fine. We'll talk about that later, when you've had time to adjust to the fact that I do it, too."

Noelle closed her eyes and groaned. "I know. I just don't want to share details."

Her mother laughed. "I won't do that. I promise." Her smile faded. "What do you want?"

"I want him to love me back. He says he can't. I think he won't. He's had so much happen in his life. His mother dying, his dad leaving." She talked a little about Jackson Hunter and his unexpected return. "Dev isn't really dealing with him, although I'm hoping they'll reconcile. After Dev's grandfather died, he was responsible for raising Jimmy and that didn't go well."

She detailed how Dev blamed himself for his brother's death.

"From what you've said, it seems to me that everyone Dev has loved has either gone away or rejected him or both," her mother told her.

Noelle hadn't thought of his past like that, but it was true. Everyone always left or died. Was that the problem? Did he think he couldn't trust anyone who cared to stick around?

"What about his romantic relationships?" her mother asked. "Did you know much about them?"

"He dated a lot of beautiful women. Never for

very long, though. Katherine told me once that he'd been engaged a few years ago. Supposedly he was crazy about her, but she wasn't willing to marry him and deal with Jimmy."

"Which means no one has been willing to stick around for Dev," her mother said slowly. "Maybe that's your answer."

"What if he won't give in? What if he won't love me back?"

"Happiness isn't a guarantee, Noelle. You have to decide what you most want and then be willing to work for it. You and Dev have only been married a few weeks. Before that, you'd barely met the man. Give it time. Have faith in him and yourself and the life you're building together."

Good advice, Noelle thought, hoping she was able to take it. "I'm sorry I lied about everything."

"I'm sorry you felt you had to. I'd say next time trust me enough to tell me the truth, but I don't think there's going to be a next time."

Noelle smiled. "I promise I'll never get into a

situation like this again. Are you going to tell Dad?"

Her mother nodded. "But not the girls. They don't need to know the details of your unusual arrangement."

"Thanks. Do you think we have a chance?"

"Yes. Don't give up on him. I like Dev and you know I think you're wonderful. Be patient and trust your heart."

"I don't have a choice," Noelle said with a sigh. "I love him and I need to be with him."

"Then you have your answer."

Dev got home from work at his usual time. He braced himself for the auditory onslaught, but the house was quiet. Oddly enough, that made him uneasy. Where was everyone?

He walked into the kitchen, but it was empty and dark. While he wasn't worried that Noelle had run off, he would feel better if she were home. Had something happened?

He glanced at the answering machine, but

the light wasn't blinking. No messages. If something had happened, she would have called. So she was at study group or the grocery store or with a friend. Maybe she and Tiffany had gone shopping.

He crossed to the refrigerator and pulled it open. The shelves were filled with leftovers, his favorite soda, snacks, ingredients for meals. Before Noelle, he could have stored his winter coat in the space and had plenty of room to spare.

She'd made changes, and not just in the kitchen. She wanted to make more changes, and that's what he couldn't let happen.

She insisted on wearing her feelings like a badge of honor. She wanted too much from him. Didn't she understand that love made a person weak?

He took a soda and popped open the can, then walked toward the bedroom to get changed. As he passed the family room, he heard an odd sound and saw Tiffany curled up on the sofa, obviously crying.

His first instinct was to run. So were his second

and third. But she'd already seen him and as much as he didn't want to deal with her tears, he couldn't be so heartless as to walk away now.

Great, he thought. This was just great. Where was Noelle? Shouldn't she be handling this?

He moved into the family room and stopped on the far side of the coffee table. "So, ah, how was your day?"

Tiffany hiccupped a sob and waved her hand.

"I can see you're upset. Do you, ah, want to talk about it?"

To his horror, she nodded.

Dev swore under his breath and sank into one of the overstuffed chairs opposite the sofa. He set down his briefcase and his drink and forced himself to lean forward to show interest when he would really rather be going through some kind of surgery without being put under.

"You were at camp today, right?" he asked. "Did something happen there?"

Tiffany blew her nose. "There's a boy and I really like him. He's been talking to me and he even asked for my number, but today I saw him kissing Amber."

The last word came out as more of a high-pitched wail. Tiffany covered her face with her hands and began to sob anew.

Dev looked around for someone to rescue him, but even the pool house looked dark and unoccupied. Just his luck that the one time he needed him, his father was gone. No, wait. His father had always been gone.

Different crisis, he thought, staring at Tiffany and knowing he was the last person to be helping her. Still, he couldn't make himself say "Why don't you wait until your sister gets home."

"What's his name?" Dev asked, stalling for time.

"Justin. He's really cute and nice and funny. I hate him and I hate Amber."

The need to bolt was so strong, Dev felt his muscles tense in anticipation. Why him? Why now?

He had no idea what to say. What could possibly comfort Tiffany? Except maybe the truth.

"How old is Justin?"

"Sixteen. He didn't really want to work in the camp this summer, he wanted to get a job. His parents said he had to for one more year, so they're paying for the insurance and stuff on his car." She drew in a shaky breath. "He talked about us driving to the beach but now I bet he's going to do that with Amber."

There were more sobs and tears.

"Look, Tiffany," he said slowly. "All teenage guys are idiots. You wake up one morning and suddenly there are girls in the world. Sure, they were always there but until that moment, you didn't care. Overnight they became beautiful and mysterious and they smell good."

She looked at him. "I don't understand."

"This is a tough time for you, right? You're changing, you're waiting to grow up, you have to make decisions about what to do with your life and you don't have a clue."

She nodded. "Why do I have to decide now?

What if I pick wrong? Noelle always knew, but she's perfect."

He ignored the sullen tone and the dig at Noelle. "Justin is feeling all that, too. Plus, he's the guy. He's expected to make the first move, which means he has to risk being rejected."

"But I'd never reject him!"

"He doesn't know that. No guy knows what's going to happen. The more special the girl, the more nervous the guy gets. A lot of times, we start with what's easy and work our way up to the hard stuff. So maybe we ask out a girl who isn't the one we're dreaming of, because it won't hurt so bad if she says no."

"You think Justin's working his way up to me?" Tiffany asked, obviously confused.

"Maybe. Or maybe he's just a guy who likes leading girls on."

"No! Justin is amazing. He'd never do that."

Dev groaned. "Tiffany, do you really know this guy? Have you spent time with him? Or are you taking one look at him and realizing you know deep in your soul exactly what he's like?"

"I just know," she breathed.

He wondered if pounding his head against a wall would make any of this easier.

"You don't know," he said as gently as he could. "You're imagining what you want him to be, but you don't know anything about him. His favorite music, his hobbies, how he treats his friends."

"But we're meant to be together. I can feel it. I love him."

"You love what you want him to be. The guy in your mind has nothing to do with Justin in real life. They may have some things in common and they may not."

Tears filled her eyes. "You're being mean on purpose."

"I'm not, Tiffany. I'm telling you the truth. If Justin flirted with you and asked for your number and now he's kissing someone else, then he's a jerk. He likes getting girls interested in him. He doesn't care about the girl, he wants the attention.

You're too special for that. You deserve a guy who's interested in you, not the chase. Wouldn't you like to be with someone who thinks you're as great as you imagine Justin to be?"

She opened her mouth, then closed it. "What?"

"Wouldn't you rather be with someone who thinks you're amazing instead of some jerk who spends his time kissing Amber?"

"There's someone who thinks I'm special?" she asked quietly.

Dev didn't doubt that Tiffany was a teenage boy's idea of paradise. She was pretty, funny, caring and outgoing. He had a feeling that once she when back to school, she was going to be swimming in potential boyfriends. "Sure. The problem is finding him and figuring out if you're interested in him."

Tiffany threw herself into his arms. "Thanks, Dev. You're right. Justin's stupid. Plus, Amber's breath always smells. Why would he want to kiss her? I like this other guy a lot better, whoever he is."

He patted her back, then hastily stood. "Glad I could help. I'm going to get changed."

"Okay." She grabbed the remote and turned on the TV. A music video blasted through the room.

Dev walked toward the hallway and was surprised to find Noelle hovering just out of sight.

"When did you get home?" he asked.

"Right around the time you asked the boy's name."

"You could have stepped in and saved me."

She smiled. "You did just fine. Why do you worry about being a good parent? You have excellent instincts."

"Right. Instincts that got my brother killed."

"You're not to blame," she said earnestly. "Dev, Jimmy made his own choices. You offered guidance and rules and consequences. He wasn't willing to learn the easy way, so he had to learn the hard way. Eventually, we all have to come to terms with what we've done."

"He didn't deserve to die," he told her. "If I'd spent more time with him or hadn't been so strict…"

"You don't know that anything would have been different. Jimmy was in trouble from the time he could walk. Maybe it was just his nature."

"Telling myself that means taking the easy way out."

"You want to take the hard way?"

"I want to do what's right. You said yourself that we all have to take responsibility for our choices. I'm taking responsibility for mine. Jimmy's death is on my hands and I can't rationalize that truth away."

"You know too many people," Rachel said under her breath as she passed yet another package.

Noelle looked at the women crowding in her parents' living room. "I kind of have to agree. I made a list for my mom, but she kept hounding me for more names. I think she invited everyone I ever met and they all said yes."

What had started out as a small postwedding shower had turned into a giant girl fest with cookies, a big mock wedding cake, fudge and, of course, diet soda.

"I'm glad I got here early," Crissy said from her spot on Noelle's other side. "I think the late-comers will be parking a mile away."

"The good news is," Rachel said with a grin, "you'll never fit all the presents in your car. That's pretty cool."

"Dev's coming over later to help me cart everything back."

Noelle couldn't believe her "haul," as Tiffany called it. Not only had every female she'd ever met come to the party, they'd all brought presents. There were mountains of boxes containing everything from place settings to flatware to crystal to a very sexy nightgown from Katherine, her former boss.

"You haven't said anything about the wedding," Kelly, a friend from high school, said. "Come on. You ran off. That's romantic. So what happened. You were hanging out one night and realized you just couldn't wait another second to be married?"

Noelle had known there would be questions

and she hadn't figured out how to answer them. "Dev and I—" she began, only to be interrupted by her mother.

"There are pictures," her mom said, waving several photos in the air. "From the wedding. I confess, I'm torn. On the one hand, I missed my firstborn getting married. On the other, I didn't have to go buy a mother-of-the-bride dress and deal with caterers."

Everyone laughed and the pictures were passed around.

"Your mom knows?" Crissy asked in a low voice.

Noelle nodded. "I confessed all a few days ago. She's been great about everything."

"Including the distractions," Crissy muttered. "Okay, I'll take the next one, and Rachel, you're in charge after that."

"Thanks," Noelle told her, then forced herself to smile as Summer pointed out she hadn't opened the present she was holding.

"Oh, look," somebody said as Noelle ripped

open more wrapping paper. "They're so in love. You can tell by how they're looking at each other."

Noelle smiled in response to the chorus of "ahh" and was grateful the picture wasn't a close-up. No doubt then the fear would be visible in her eyes. As it was, she didn't even remember posing for pictures after the short ceremony.

She hated lying to everyone, but under the circumstances, standing up and announcing the truth didn't seem like such a good idea, either. Her mother had put together the shower before she'd found out why Noelle had married Dev, and once she knew, it was too late to cancel without a lot of awkward explanations.

With help from her friends, she continued opening presents and smiling. An hour or so later, Dev arrived and was instantly surrounded by women eager to congratulate him on his recent marriage and to ask him if he had any single friends.

Noelle escaped to the kitchen on the pretext

of getting more cookies. When she reached for one of the trays, she found Dev next to her.

"How are you holding up?" he asked.

"I'm fine."

"You don't look fine. You look upset."

She shrugged. "I don't like lying to everyone. They think we ran off because we were wildly in love. I even thought about telling them the truth, but I don't want that information out there. Eventually we'll have to tell the baby what really happened, but that's a conversation that we should have when we're ready. Not because the local gossips are hinting at it."

"Do their opinions really matter?" he asked.

"I don't like feeling like a fraud. It wouldn't be so bad if we could admit what we did and why, but then tell everyone that it's okay now, because we fell in love with each other. But we didn't, did we? You don't."

He looked uncomfortable. "I've explained."

"No, you haven't. Not in any way I can understand. So here's another question in my long list of them. How long, Dev? How long will it take for you to give in? I know it's a mountain and I'm willing to make the climb. I'm just curious. Is it a beginning level and I just have to walk for a few weeks, or are we talking Mount Everest and I'm not even at base camp?"

"I don't know how to answer that."

She picked up a tray of cookies. "I disagree. I think you know exactly what I'm up against, but you don't want to tell me."

By the time they'd unloaded all the presents from both cars, they'd filled the entire living room with boxes and bags of gifts.

"You're gonna be writing thank-you notes for days," Tiffany said, sounding awed by the bounty. "Where are you going to put everything?"

"I have no idea."

Dev wasn't sure, either. "We'll have to clear out a few closets. Maybe some in the hall. I think the buffet in the dining room is empty. We could put the china in there."

"We got service for sixteen," Noelle said, sounding shell-shocked by the concept. "I don't know how to cook for sixteen."

"We don't have to have that many over. Or anyone."

"I'm going to bed," Tiffany said. "'Night."

She walked down the hall. It wasn't that late. Dev wondered if she were trying to make sure she didn't get stuck unpacking.

Noelle looked at all the boxes. "I can't deal with this now. How about we work on this in the morning?"

"Fine with me."

"I need something to eat," she said. "Something that doesn't have sugar in it."

Once in the kitchen she got out bread and sliced meat. "Want anything?" she asked.

He shook his head.

She moved with a familiarity that told him how thoroughly she'd become a part of his life and how much he'd changed hers. While the former was a good thing, the later was less easily defined.

"I did all this to make things easier," he said. "That was always my goal."

She pulled a jar of mustard from the refrigerator. "I know," she told him, not pretending to misunderstand. "You're good about doing the right thing."

"I didn't mean to hurt you."

"You don't."

How was that possible? If she loved him, didn't his inability to return the emotion cause her pain?

"You don't hurt me," she insisted quietly. "Not in the way you mean. You're not doing anything wrong. You're following the rules as you wrote them. I went my own way and these are the consequences. It hurts, but I don't see you as the cause."

That surprised him. How could she let him off so easily?

But she wasn't finished.

"What I do blame you for," she continued, "is trying to make things easier for yourself rather than me. Marrying me is a by-product of what you want. You made the safe choice. You always make the safe choice."

"Wait a minute. How is marrying you safe?"

Her blue eyes darkened with emotion. "You thought you could have it all. A wife, a child, a marriage and nothing messy. You spelled out all possibilities and dealt with them. When this ended, I was supposed to go my way and you would go yours. Neither of us would look back. You got to have it all and never risk your heart."

"I married you because of the baby," he said, doing his best to keep his temper in check. She didn't know what she was talking about.

"You're afraid to love," she said. "With all that's happened to you, I can see why, but that doesn't change the fact that you're a coward."

"I see," he said icily. "So working my ass off, raising my brother the best I can, cleaning up his messes even after he's dead makes me a coward."

Her face paled. Instantly he realized what he'd said and how she would have felt about it. Guilt sliced through him.

"I'm sorry," he told her sincerely. "I didn't mean that the way it came out. You know I didn't."

"It's fine." Her voice was thick with pain. "It's good to know where I stand. Just another of Jimmy's messes." She closed her eyes for a moment, then opened them. "I take it back, Dev. You have hurt me."

He took a step toward her. "I didn't mean to. I didn't mean for any of this to happen. Not the way it did."

"What did you mean?"

"I meant…" Damn. What could he say? Initially he had thought of her as little more than a problem to be solved.

"How long have you been hiding behind the right thing?" she asked. "How long has responsibility kept you safe? I know why you didn't get married before. You had Jimmy to hide behind. Your ex-fiancée didn't run, you pushed her away."

"You're wrong," he said harshly. "You don't understand." She couldn't know what it had been like to be the only one who was willing to do the right thing. She had no idea what it had cost him.

"I understand everything. You used Jimmy to protect yourself from love. You believe that love makes you weak, but you're wrong. It makes you strong and powerful. Giving our hearts is the most courageous thing we can do. I admired you for so long and now I see you're just afraid. You're not willing to make the effort, to take a chance."

Her words were a light shining in a dark corner. He suddenly saw himself as one of those guys he'd described to Tiffany—one of the ones who wasn't worth it.

He had no way to defend himself. He had used his brother to hold the world at bay. He'd used circumstances and the company and everything else he could think of because loving meant being left yet again.

They stared at each other for a long time. Finally he broke the silence.

"I wanted to make it right," he told her. "I wanted

to make things easier for you. Instead I've only made them more difficult. I'm sorry. I'll go."

Her expression tightened. "You're leaving me?"

"You have your family. You won't be alone."

"You're leaving," she repeated, not asking a question this time. "I can't believe it. You screw this up and your answer is to run?"

"I'll still take responsibility," he said.

"Of course you do. That's what you do best. But what if I want you to show up? That's a whole different story, isn't it?" She threw up both her hands. "Go. Just go. Don't worry about the responsibility, Dev. In case you haven't noticed, I'm good at that, too. I don't need anyone else to be in charge or handle the details. I need a partner. I need someone willing to love me back."

She was the strongest, most incredible person he'd ever met. He'd come into this relationship with a list of rules he thought would protect him, but now, faced with losing her, he realized that all the rules in the world weren't going to help.

But she didn't see the truth. What if he stayed? What if he allowed himself to love her? He would be weak and then what would she have?

"I'll stay through the weekend," he said.

"Don't bother. If you're going, go now."

Noelle watched Dev pack. Each item he put in the suitcase felt like a slap. She couldn't believe he was really doing this. Leaving. Walking out. Not even trying first.

After a couple of minutes, she figured out she couldn't stand to see this.

"There is some irony," she told him from the doorway. "Despite not spending a lot of time with your father, you're amazingly like him. Here you are, walking out on your family when we need you the most."

She didn't wait for an answer. Instead she went outside and sat by the pool.

The night was cool and quiet. She could hear the TV in Tiffany's room and music coming from the pool house. She also heard the garage door open, Dev's car back out and then the garage door close.

She sat alone in the silence and told herself she would be fine. She wondered how long it would take before she could believe it.

Chapter Thirteen

Both Crissy and Rachel responded to Noelle's early morning calls for help. They all met up at Rachel's apartment. As it was summer, Rachel wasn't working and Crissy took the morning off.

"I can't believe he's gone," Noelle said, trying desperately not to cry. She'd spent most of the night in tears and was determined to be done with them. "I know I pushed, but I thought he would push back. I thought he'd care enough to fight for me."

Crissy and Rachel sat on each side of her, rubbing her back and offering her tissue.

"I know this is hard," Crissy said, "but you did the right thing. The rules have changed. Dev not acknowledging that doesn't change the truth of the situation. You're not where you were. This is no longer a sensible business arrangement."

"I don't get it," Rachel said. "You love him. You're having his brother's baby, you're great together, you have a terrific family. Why wouldn't he want to be with you? It's like he finally got everything he wants and now he's running from it."

There was a wistful quality to Rachel's voice. Noelle remembered that her friend had lost her entire family when she'd been twelve and had been raised in foster care. Noelle guessed that Rachel would give anything to be a part of a family willing to claim her as their own.

"I know I did the right thing," Noelle said. "I just wish it didn't hurt so much."

"He'll come around," Rachel said.

Noelle looked at her. "Are you sure? Because I'm not."

"He's not a stupid man," Rachel said. "He's afraid, but give him time. I don't think he can resist you for very long."

"And if he isn't, you can hunt him down like the rodent he is," Crissy said cheerfully.

Despite everything, Noelle smiled. "I don't want to hurt him."

"Too bad, because that would make you feel better."

Noelle laughed, then groaned in frustration when the laughter turned to tears. "I'm not doing this anymore," she said as she wiped her face. "I'm done crying over him."

Crissy and Rachel exchanged a glance. "Do you want us to say he's a jerk?" Crissy asked.

"I don't think it will help," Noelle admitted. "That's the worst of it. He's *not* a total loser. I know he's going to be there for the baby and me. He'll take responsibility, because that's what he does best. He'll change diapers and help with baths and do everything right except love me." She swallowed. "What if it's not just me? What if he won't love the baby, either?"

"He loved Jimmy," Rachel said. "The baby will be his family. He can't escape that."

Maybe Dev couldn't escape, Noelle thought sadly, but he'd just proved to her he could run. What happened the next time things got hard? Would he be like his father and take off forever?

Everything she knew about him told her she could trust him, but until last night, she would never have guessed he could walk out on her the way he had. If she'd been wrong before, chances are she could be wrong again.

Dev found himself spending lots of time at the office, but he wasn't getting any work done. He missed Noelle. No, that wasn't right. He *ached* for her and he still didn't know what had happened between them. When had everything gone so wrong?

He lived his day knowing leaving had been the right thing, but wanting desperately to go back to her. But how could he if he couldn't give her the one thing she wanted most? He refused to let her live a life of unhappiness, the way his mother had.

There had been times when—

The door to his office opened and his father walked in. Dev rose to his feet, intent on getting rid of the man as quickly as possible, then he sank back into his seat. What was the point? He'd screwed up every other relationship in his life, maybe it was time to confess all and screw up this one, too.

"I'd ask how it's going," his father said as he settled in a chair across from Dev's. "Only I can imagine. She's upset, you're upset. This really sucks."

The summation would have been humorous if it hadn't been so accurate and painful. "It's all my fault," Dev said.

"I doubt that." His father sipped on the cup of

coffee he'd brought in with him. "It generally takes two to mess up a relationship."

"Not in this case," Dev said, then drew in a breath. "Not with Jimmy, either."

He told his father what had happened to his youngest son. How Jimmy had been in and out of trouble, how he, Dev, had tried to convince him to change his ways. How in the end, Dev had given him a choice of military service or jail. How he'd been responsible for Jimmy's death.

When he was finished, his father gazed at him for a long time.

"I was right there with you, son, until that last bit." He took another sip of the coffee. "Jimmy always chose the hardest path. I could see it, even when he was five or six. He hated rules, he tested everyone around him. If there was an easy way and a hard way, Jimmy found the hard way."

"I'm the one who issued the ultimatum," Dev said, wishing for the millionth time he could have that moment back.

"You didn't steal for him and you didn't shoot

him. Dev, Jimmy's course was set a long time ago. You couldn't save him by staying and I couldn't save him by leaving."

Dev stared at his father. "What are you talking about?"

"I left because of Jimmy. I thought maybe if I wasn't around to be a bad influence, he'd do better. My father said he could make things right with Jimmy and I believed him."

"That's not true," Dev said angrily. "You said you were leaving so I wouldn't turn out like you. I was the reason you left."

His father frowned. "Noelle mentioned something about that. I…" The older man swore. "Dev, I am so sorry. You were sharing a room. Do you remember? Jimmy was having nightmares after his mother died, so we put that air mattress into your room. The night I came to say goodbye, I was talking to Jimmy, not you."

Dev didn't have to close his eyes to remember that night. It had been late, well after midnight, and he'd awakened to find his father standing in the doorway. The hall light had been on and his father's face had been in shadow. Dev hadn't been able to read his dad's expression, but he still remembered the pain of his father's words. Words not even meant for him.

"I thought you left because of me," he repeated slowly.

His father half rose, then sank back into his chair. "That explains a lot. I wondered why you never wrote me back. I knew you'd be angry and hurt because of my leaving. I just didn't know…" Jackson Hunter suddenly looked old and broken.

"Why would I ever worry about you turning out like me?" his father asked. "You're too much like your grandfather for that to happen."

There was something about the way he made the statement. "Didn't you and your father get along?"

Jackson laughed. "About as well as you and Jimmy. He wanted me to follow in his footsteps. To be responsible and take over the company. I wasn't interested in that." He shrugged. "Or anything. I lacked ambition. Your grandfather couldn't forgive that."

Dev couldn't get his mind around the information. From the time he was sixteen years old, he'd defined himself by his father's words. To not turn out like him. But as he hadn't known what his father meant, the path had been shaded and confusing.

"I screwed up," his father said. "By trying not to screw up, I made things worse. I'm sorry, Dev. If I'd known, I would have stayed and..." He paused and took a sip of his coffee. "Sorry, no. That's crap. I would have left anyway."

"Because of Mom?"

His father nodded. "That's *my* guilt."

"You didn't love her," Dev said, confident of this fact. "Why didn't you? It was all she ever wanted."

He didn't want to say more, or accuse too strongly. He had his own demons in the not-loving department.

"I did love her," his father said slowly. "As much as I could. But it wasn't enough. She was a black hole of emotion. She wanted to suck the life out of me and even that wasn't enough. Early on, I thought her neediness was charming. It made me feel like a man to take care of her. But after a while, I found I couldn't breathe without being strangled."

Dev didn't know what to say. His father's words had nothing to do with the warm, loving memories he had. His mother had always been there for him. She'd waited until he got home from school and then she'd wanted them to be together constantly until his father got home. They'd played games and talked.

He frowned. Now that he thought about it, he realized his mother hadn't wanted him to bring friends home, nor had she liked him to go hang out at someone else's house. Abut the time he'd started to rebel against that, Jimmy had been old enough to claim his mother's attention with his activities.

"No matter what I did, it wasn't enough," his father said. "She slowly cut me off from my friends until she was the only one I saw. I knew we'd reached the end when she admitted that she wanted me to quit my job and stay home with her twenty-four hours a day. I knew that was a symptom of something being very wrong. I tried to get her help but she refused. So I ran. Emotionally at least."

Dev nodded slowly. He'd been about twelve or thirteen when his father had pretty much stopped showing up at home. That's when his mother started to go downhill. He remembered hearing her crying all night, waiting for a man who wasn't coming back.

"I took the easy way out," his father said. "I'm not proud of that. I let you and Jimmy down, I let my father down, although he was used to that. He'd been disappointed in me since the day I was born."

"Dad, no," Dev said.

"It's true. I didn't care about the company, I wasn't interested in finance or engineering or any part of the business. Oh, I liked the money well enough. I still do. Those monthly checks keep me going."

Dev didn't know what to do with all the information. There had been too much in too short a period of time.

"You've done well," his father said unexpectedly. "For what it's worth, I'm proud of you. Your grandfather would have been proud, too. You've grown his company in ways he never could."

"I… Don't be proud of me," Dev told him.

His father sighed impatiently. "Dammit, Dev, quit being a martyr. If you have to claim some trait from your mother, for God's sake pick something else. You didn't kill your brother."

Dev stood. "You don't know what you're talking about."

"Of course I do. Let it go, or the guilt will kill you. You're not like me. You can't turn your back on the people you've hurt and still live your life. It'll eat you up inside. You've got something good with Noelle. Drop the past and move on."

Dev sank back into the chair. "I don't have Noelle."

"Of course you do. She loves you. Anyone can see that."

"It's not what you think. The reason I married her, I mean." He quickly told the story of Noelle's relationship with Jimmy and subsequent pregnancy.

"It's a marriage of convenience," Dev concluded.

His father looked surprised by the information but he recovered quickly. "It may have started out that way, but it isn't anymore. She loves you and I think you love her. Only you're acting like a jackass. An unfortunate trait you get from me. The good news is Noelle's heart is bigger than her sense of self-preservation. You haven't blown it completely. You can still get her back."

"What if I don't want her back?"

"Then you're a fool. You won't do better."

"I don't expect to do better. I expect her to find someone who can be all she needs."

His father finished his coffee and tossed the container into the trash by the desk. "You're willing to let another man touch her and tell her he loves her? You're willing to let someone else raise Jimmy's child."

Dev's chest tightened. He didn't want any of that. He especially didn't want Noelle curled up in another bed, laughing after an amazing night of lovemaking. He didn't want her making peanut butter cookies for another man, or talking about her day or…

"If I love her, then I'll break," he said quietly.

"Love isn't for sissies," his father told him. "So you break. Noelle helps you put the pieces back together and you move on."

"As simple as that," Dev said, refusing to believe it was possible.

"Why make it complicated? You found an amazing woman, Dev. You got lucky. You've always been smart. Why be stupid now?"

"You make it sound so easy."

"It's not. But it's worth it."

"Have you been in love?" Dev asked.

His father nodded. "Twice. Once with your mother, until she crushed the feeling out of me, and once a few years ago. But she belonged to someone else and she wouldn't consider leaving him. Love doesn't come along all that often. When it does, you should grab on with both hands and never let go."

Noelle had yet to get used to having Dev gone. With Tiffany around, the house was never quiet, but there was definitely something missing. At night her bed seemed too big for one person and she couldn't seem to get to sleep. Pathetically, she'd taken to wearing one of Dev's T-shirts instead of pjs, so that she could pretend to be close to him.

She felt emotionally exhausted. So much had happened in the past few weeks. She'd been living a roller-coaster life and part of her just wanted to get off and slow down for a while. But that scenario didn't include having Dev walk out on her. Instead, she would prefer that the two of them were together, falling deeper in love, discovering how great it was to be married.

"Stupid fantasy," she murmured as she whipped up a batch of brownies on Thursday morning.

She'd just put the glass pan into the oven, when Tiffany walked into the kitchen and announced, "I'm leaving. I'm going back home. Mom's coming to pick me up in an hour."

Noelle was torn between amusement at her sister's self-made drama and the uncomfortable realization that she was one person closer to being totally alone.

"Okay," she said. "I've enjoyed having you here."

"I guess I have to thank you for letting me stay," Tiffany said, not sounding the least bit gracious. "But you weren't very fun. There are too many rules here. Even Mom doesn't have this many rules."

Noelle didn't bother pointing out that she and her mother had exactly the same rules. If Tiffany needed that as an excuse to go home, Noelle was all for it.

"Are you all packed?" she asked her sister. "Do you need any help?"

Tiffany's eyes filled with tears. "You're happy to see me go, aren't you? You've hated having me here."

"What? No." Noelle moved close and touched her arm. "Tiff, I've really liked having you here. It's been fun being in the same house again. I've missed that. I'm not trying to push you out. I just know that when you've made up your mind, it's made up. My offer to help you pack was just that. An offer to help."

Tiffany didn't look convinced. "You shouldn't be like that. All stiff and full of rules. I know it's why Dev left."

Noelle knew her sister was lashing out, hurting in return for being hurt. It didn't matter that Noelle hadn't meant to wound. Still, the words did what they were supposed to.

"Dev left for a lot of complicated reasons," she said quietly.

"He left because you have too many rules and you're no fun. He was hardly ever home. He didn't want to be around you."

Tiffany's angry outburst articulated every one of Noelle's personal fears. She ached inside for what she'd wanted and lost without ever having.

"You don't know what you're talking about," Noelle told her.

"See," Tiffany said. "You don't even care that he's gone. You're not crying. Why aren't you crying?"

It was too difficult to explain that there weren't any tears left. Not for Dev or their relationship. Noelle wasn't sure how to fix things because she was still having trouble figuring out the problem.

"This isn't about you," Noelle said. "This is about Dev and me. I'm not going to talk about it."

"He left because of me, didn't he?" Tiffany asked as she sank onto the floor. "I was too much trouble. It's all my fault."

Noelle sighed. Of course. Her sister was all bravado, but behind that brave face was a typical, confused teenager.

She crouched down and pulled Tiffany close. "Dev's leaving had nothing to do with you. Even if you'd never been born, he would have gone away."

Tiffany stared at her. "Promise?"

Noelle kissed the top of her head. "Cross my heart."

"He shouldn't have left. That wasn't very nice. Mom says all newly married couples have problems and the only way to work them out is to live through them."

"Good advice."

"You should tell Dev. Or have Mom talk to him. Then he'll come back and you can be happy again."

"An interesting idea," Noelle said, not yet ready to send her mother in to clean up this mess. "Whatever happens with Dev, you don't have to go if you don't want to."

Tiffany sniffed. "I've had a good time being with you, but I kinda miss home. You know, my room and stuff. Plus, there's only a few more weeks until Lily leaves for college and I'd like to spend time with her and Summer." She shifted onto her knees. "I know. With Dev gone, you could move back, too. It could be like before."

Noelle glanced at her wedding band. "It can never be like it was before. I'm married now." And pregnant, she thought, knowing it was about time to tell everyone there would be a baby in the new year.

Tiffany sighed. "I always thought growing up would be really cool, but it isn't always, is it?"

Noelle smiled at her. "Honestly, sometimes being an adult is a total drag."

Noelle tried to read a magazine in the doctor's office, but she couldn't focus. Her appointment was for her first ultrasound and she was five different kinds of nervous.

Logically she knew everything was fine. Why

wouldn't it be? But this was new and strange and scary and she was by herself.

She'd thought about asking her mom to come along, but she'd started a new job only a couple of weeks before and Noelle didn't want her to have to take time off so soon. When the appointment had been made, Noelle had assumed Dev would be with her. That would have been plenty of moral support.

She set down the magazine and picked up another one with a cute baby on the cover. Her child was growing inside of her. She still had virtually no symptoms except for the fact that her stomach was getting bigger. She kept waiting for morning sickness or breast tenderness, but so far, nothing.

The door to the waiting room opened. Noelle glanced up, then nearly fell off her chair when Dev walked in. He crossed to where she was sitting and took the chair next to hers.

"You're here," she said, and then felt foolish for stating the obvious.

"You have an appointment. I wanted to be with you for the ultrasound."

He looked different, she thought as she stared at his face, noting shadows that hadn't been there before. Did he look thinner and more tired? Or was she just hoping that he was missing her?

Maybe she was an idiot, but she couldn't help being happy to see him. She wanted to touch him and talk to him. She wanted to know everything he'd been doing. It felt as if they'd been apart a year instead of six days.

"How are you doing?" he asked. "Are you feeling all right?"

"I'm good. Busy with my class. Tiffany moved out. Apparently she finally missed home."

What she really wanted to say was that she missed him with a desperation that couldn't be explained in just words. That she wanted him back home, in her life and in her bed. That she would try to love him a little less if he would try to love her a little more and maybe they could meet in the middle.

Instead she asked, "How are you doing?"

"Good. I have suppliers in from China. I've been in meetings with them most of the week." He glanced at his watch. "Katherine is taking them on a tour of the city and we're getting back together when I'm done here."

He sounded busy. "You didn't have to come."

He took her hand. "I wanted to. Noelle, there are some things I need to talk to you about. I've been doing a lot of thinking."

Her chest gave a little squeeze of hope. "About good things or bad things?" she asked.

He smiled. "Important things. My suppliers are leaving tomorrow. Can I come by in the afternoon and we'll talk?"

Only if he was going to tell her that he wanted to try again. She didn't think she could handle him suggesting they get a divorce now.

"I'll be home," she said. "Can you give me a hint as to the topic?"

Just then a nurse stepped into the waiting room and called her name.

Timing, Noelle thought glumly. Life was all about timing.

* * *

Twenty minutes later Noelle was on the table with Dev at her side, clutching her hand as tightly as she was clutching his.

"Okay, we're going to go through this slowly," the technician said. "I'll explain what we're seeing." She smiled. "It's not always intuitive. And to answer the question I nearly always get on a first ultrasound, yes, that's really a baby."

She showed them the baby's head and spine. "It's too early to know the gender, but you two need to decide if you want to know in advance or not."

Noelle looked at Dev. "What do you think?"

He shook his head. "I'm still grasping the fact that we're having a baby. It's real."

She smiled. "Soon we'll have the dirty diapers to prove it."

The technician hesitated, then set down her wand. "I'll be right back."

She left. Noelle stared at the now blank monitor. "I don't know who thought this machine up, but it's great. I can't wait until I'm further along and we can see more of the baby. I can't decide about the gender thing. It would be nice to have the room ready, but I also like the idea of a surprise."

Dev bent down and kissed her. Anything else she'd planned on saying flew out of her brain.

The technician returned, along with the doctor.

"All right," the doctor said. "Now I want you both to take a deep breath. I'm sure everything is fine." She picked up the wand and turned on the screen, then moved the wand over Noelle's stomach.

Noelle felt a sudden rush of cold. "You're saying something could be wrong with the baby? It's not growing right?"

Dev's fingers tightened around her own. She looked at him and saw fear in his eyes.

"I don't know," her doctor admitted. "To be sure, I'd like to do an amniocentesis. Are you familiar with that? The results take about three to four weeks and will let us know if everything is all right."

Noelle stared at Dev. This couldn't be happening, she thought frantically. Not the baby.

"It's going to be fine," he told her, looking into her eyes with such incredible focus, she knew he could actually will it to be true.

"I'm scared."

"Me, too. But we're in this together."

Noelle still felt numb with shock as she and Dev left the doctor's office. They'd been reassured that everything was probably all right and better to be safe and all that, but she wasn't feeling very safe.

"I'll follow you home," Dev said as he pulled out his cell phone.

"What?" She looked at him. "I'm okay."

"You're not. I'll call Katherine and explain I won't be coming back. She can handle our suppliers for the rest of the day."

As much as Noelle would have liked the company, she also felt a strong need to be alone. To figure out what all this meant to her.

"I'm fine," she said. "Really. I just want to go home and rest for a while. You go ahead and deal with your people. We can talk another time."

"I don't think you should be by yourself."

She forced herself to smile. Strength was required, she told herself. For all she knew, Dev had been planning to tell her he was never coming back.

"There's nothing either of us can do," she pointed out. "We can't change what is happening with the baby. We'll find out when the results are in. In the meantime, I'm going to assume everything is fine and live my life. You go back to work."

"You can't mean that."

"Of course I do. I'm seriously all right, Dev. I promise."

He didn't look like he believed her, but he did put away his cell phone. "I still want to come over tomorrow."

"That's fine. I'll be home all afternoon."

He walked her to her car, then kissed her

cheek. "If you change your mind, call me. I'll be right there."

"I appreciate that, but don't worry. Go."

She gave him a little push toward his car, then slid into her own. As he walked away, she felt the fear return. It crashed over her, draining her of everything but the ability to breathe and wait. How would she ever survive three or four weeks of not knowing?

Dev turned back to look at her. She gave him a smile and a wave and wondered when, exactly, she'd turned into such a good liar.

Chapter Fourteen

Noelle managed to get through the day without too much trouble, but night was another matter. She put off getting into bed until she was exhausted, but the second she lay down on the cool, clean sheets, her entire body went on alert.

Her heart raced, her head filled with questions and fear claimed her. It moved through her body like a living creature, stealing away breath and hope and will. She knew she had to fight the sensation, that she had to stay strong and try to relax, but it was impossible.

What if something was wrong with the baby? She was pretty sure she could stand anything but losing it. Medical problems could be fixed. Other kinds of problems could be dealt with. But not having a baby at all was unbearable.

She turned onto her side and curled up as tightly as she could, as if she could use the rest of her body to shield what was growing inside. She felt lost and alone and knew nothing would ever be all right until she heard from the doctor with good news.

"Please God," she prayed silently over and over. "Let everything be okay with the baby. Please."

She waited for the peace that usually followed her quiet, spiritual times, but there was only the low-grade gnawing that drained her of everything but terror. She'd left on a lamp on the nightstand, but even the soft glow in the room did nothing to chase away the shadows in her heart.

She fought against tears. To give in now would be to let the fear win. Strong, she told herself. She would be strong and powerful. The reality was, she didn't know anything, so why assume the worst?

But it was hard to be brave, so very hard. She ached inside and out. She felt cold and lost and—

The bedroom door opened. Before she could react, she saw Dev enter the room.

He crossed to the bed, kicked off his shoes, then joined her on the mattress. Without saying anything, he gathered her in his arms and held her close.

"You're not alone," he whispered. "I'm here, too. We'll get through this the same way we started. Together."

He felt warm and strong and alive. She let herself hold on to him, her head resting on his shoulder, her legs comfortably trapped by his.

"I'm scared," she admitted. "Really, really scared."

"Me, too. I shouldn't have gone back to work. I should have been here for you."

"I was okay until I came to bed."

"I wasn't," he told her. "I couldn't concentrate. I kept thinking about you and the baby and wondering if I made this happen by thinking this was just another one of Jimmy's messes I had to clean up."

She raised her head and looked at him. "Life isn't like that. Not only doesn't the universe punish you for what you think, you simply don't have that much power. You can't think something wrong or better. Things simply are."

"I know that in my head," he said. "I'm sorry I said it to you. I'm sorry I thought it in the first place. For a long time the baby wasn't real to me. It was a fact, something to handle. But not a real person."

She understood that. For her the baby had been an intellectual exercise, too. "Things changed," she said.

He nodded. "That first visit to the doctor made the baby real. It also terrified me. I wasn't ready to be a father. Not because I don't want to be tied down, but because I don't want to mess up. I want to do everything right."

"That's not going to happen. None of us is perfect. We make mistakes. The point is to never stop trying to be the best we can be. Especially when there's a child in the mix."

"You are the wisest person I know," he told her.

She managed a smile. "Then you need to get out more."

He chuckled. "I mean it. You're amazing. I loved my brother and I'm sorry he's gone, but if he'd lived and you two had gotten married, he never would have realized how lucky he was."

Her heart fluttered and for the first time in several hours, it wasn't with fear. "We might have made it."

"I don't want to think about that," Dev admitted. "I don't want to think about you with someone else. What if you had married Jimmy? We would have met and become friends. I would have thought you were great."

"I would have thought the same," she admitted, not sure where the conversation was going, but wanting to be there for the ride.

"But you would have been focused on him and I would have been…" He touched her cheek. "I would have been screwed. I would have woken up one morning and realized I was completely and totally in love with the woman married to my brother."

She forgot to breathe. "Dev…"

His dark gaze locked with hers. "I love you, Noelle. I'm sorry I was such an idiot about everything. That it took me so long to figure things out. I can give you all the reasons, if you'd like."

Hope grew. The white light of it burned away the fear. "The reasons would be nice," she said.

He smiled. "You deserve them. Okay, for the longest time I've thought that love makes a person weak. I thought my mother died of a broken heart. I'd forgotten how she'd twisted love in her mind until there was only duty and service. I'd forgotten how grateful I was when she died and I didn't have to feel guilty all the time about not pleasing her enough. Then I felt horrible for wanting her gone and I thought I'd had something to do with her getting sick. I never sat down and worked it out. I just had undefined feelings that made me uncomfortable about getting close."

He tucked her hair behind her ears. "Jimmy was another complication. I didn't know what to do with him. How to make him better. My dad says some people are just born to take the hard road and that Jimmy's one of them. I still have to think on that. But the message I still got from that was love makes you weak. Then I met you."

"Technically we ran into each other."

"That's right. And I'll be grateful for the rest of my life. Noelle, you have shown me that real love makes a person strong. Your power comes from faith and love. It always has. I don't know why you've chosen to love me, but I don't want that to ever change. I'm sorry for what I put you through and I hope you can forgive me. I'm willing to work at proving myself. Just tell me what you want me to do."

If she hadn't been held in his arms, she might

have floated away. "You don't have to do anything," she said. "Except promise to move back and never go away again."

"That's it?" He almost sounded disappointed.

"You have to promise to love me forever and always be willing to keep our marriage strong."

"Done." He stared at her. "Just like that? No other tests?"

"I don't want to test you, Dev. I just want us to be together. You had to find your way here on your path, just like I did. What matters to me is that we're here and we're together."

"I don't deserve you," he said, then kissed her.

Their lips met as if to seal a promise each had made. She felt his love wash over her, healing her dark places and pushing back the last of the fear.

"We'll get through this," he said, moving his hand to her belly. "Whatever happens, we'll deal with it together."

"I know. With you here, I can stand whatever happens."

His dark eyes brightened with determination. "This baby is going to be fine. So is the next and the next."

She smiled. "How many are you planning?"

"I'm not sure. How many do you want?"

"Let's start with two and work our way up from there."

He pulled her close. "Never leave me. I couldn't survive that."

"I won't," she promised. "You're my world. Why would I want to be anywhere else?"

"Then you'll marry me?"

She held up her left hand, then pointed at his. "I hate to break this to you, but we're already married."

"We got married for a lot of reasons, but none of them were about being in love and wanting to commit to each other. I want a real marriage, Noelle. I want it lousy and messy and passionate and imperfect. I want to fight and make up and have plans and build a life that makes us happy every day."

His words touched her deep inside. "I want that, too. But I'm not sure about getting married."

He looked so shocked, she started to laugh. "I'm kidding," she said. "Yes, I want to be married to you."

"You'd better be," he growled, then kissed her again. "I love you."

"I love you, too," she said. "You're exactly where I've always wanted to be."

Epilogue

Eighteen months later

The cake was impossibly large for a one-year-old child, Noelle thought humorously, yet little Mindy was far more interested in impressing everyone with her ability to walk and her ability to speak…sort of.

She was also distracted by the constant bursts of laughter from the teenage contingent across the yard.

"Don't you even think of growing up," Noelle

said, sweeping her daughter up into her arms and raining kisses on her cheeks and forehead. "You're going to be my little girl forever."

"If only," her mother said as she carried out a tray of sandwiches. "Enjoy this time. It all goes so fast. I still remember your first birthday."

Her mother got a little misty which, now that she was a mother herself, Noelle completely understood.

The Sunday afternoon was surprisingly warm for March, which was why they'd been able to hold the celebration outside. Now Mindy squirmed to get down, then walked to her grandmother and held up both her arms.

"Up," the little girl said. "G'ma up."

"Did you say Grandma?" Noelle's mother picked up the toddler and swung her in a circle. "Bob," she called to where the guys were standing around the barbecue and talking. "She said grandma."

Noelle's father grumbled. "She still likes me best."

"Of course she does, dear. I think we need to

get more pictures. Come on, you sweet little angel. Let's go inside and get the camera. There can never be too many pictures of my very first granddaughter, can there?"

Mindy laughed.

Noelle watched them go into the house. She felt deep contentment and a sense of everything in her world being where it should be.

After three grueling weeks of waiting for the results of the amniocentesis, the time made bearable only by Dev's constant and devoted presence, they'd learned that the baby was perfectly healthy in every way. Mindy had arrived right on time and she'd grown into a bright, happy little girl.

Dev walked over and put his arm around her. "What are you thinking?"

"That we have a very good life." She nodded at his father. "I'm glad Jackson bought that house down the street. I like having him close."

"Me, too," Dev said. "Although what he's going to do with a place that big is beyond me."

"He might get married again."

"That would be good. I'd like him to find someone."

They'd come so far, she thought happily. She had graduated from community college in January, on schedule, and had already started at UC Riverside. Her classload was light enough to let her spend plenty of time with Mindy. When her daughter had to be left with someone, Noelle used the church day care or one of the many volunteers. There was her mother, Dev's father, or her sisters.

Dev had provided all three of her sisters with college scholarships, allowing her mother to go back to the work she loved at the church.

"We're very blessed," she said.

Dev hugged her close. "Yes, we are."

She smiled. "I know it's Mindy's birthday, but I have a present for you."

He raised his eyebrows. "I had my present last night."

"You can have it again tonight, if you want,

but this is something different." She paused. "Actually, I guess they're related."

"Are you going to tell me what you're talking about?" he asked teasingly. "Or do I have to guess?"

"I'll tell you." She took his hand and placed it on her stomach. "I'm thinking September. Maybe this time we'll have a boy."

Dev swept her up in his arms and swung her around. Then he set her on the ground and kissed her so thoroughly, she felt light-headed. Around them, no one paid attention. Their families were used to this kind of display.

She and Dev would share their happy news later, she thought as her husband kissed her again. Mindy would enjoy being a big sister.

Sometimes, she thought happily, life really was a miracle.

* * * * *